Hemiplegic Utopia – Manc Style

Living with Hemiplegia

by

Lee Seymour

Augur Press

British Library Cataloguing in Publication Data.
A catalogue record for this book is available from the British Library.

ISBN 978-0-9549551-7-5

First published 2008 by
Augur Press
Delf House
52, Penicuik Road,
Roslin,
Midlothian EH25 9LH
United Kingdom

Printed and bound by CPI Antony Rowe, Eastbourne.

Hemiplegic Utopia – Manc Style

Living with Hemiplegia

Acknowledgements

Thanks to my mum for always being there for me through thick and thin. This one's for you!

Thanks to Paul for being my little brother. I told you I'd make you proud of me one day!

Thanks to Craig for not letting me give up on my dreams.

Thanks to John and Ewan for nearly fifteen years of friendship.

Thanks to Boonie Boy for advice on life. I hope I'll meet you one day!

Thanks to Joseph for keeping my feet firmly on the ground throughout this whole process.

Thanks to Lou for believing that this day would come. You know me inside out like no other woman!

Thanks to Mirabelle for making a goal reality.

Thanks to Ian, John, Mani and Reni for inspiring quiet confidence in me. Your no-nonsense music during the bad days meant that I ignored those doubters who claimed this book would never come into being.

Thanks to Jessie, whose belief in me before passing over helped me to see this project through.

And thanks to Natalie and Rebekah for the impact of their short lives upon mine.

Contents

Introduction

Introduction

Lee entered the world on 21st April 1980 at 4.35 p.m., fists clenched on the top of his head making it a difficult birth. Maybe this was a sign that there was a tricky life ahead, and maybe he had some instinctive sense of this, and was trying to delay his delivery a little longer.

It was only when he was eight months old that doctors diagnosed that he was suffering from hemiplegia, and all his life he has struggled because of considerable paralysis of his left side due to the presence of two centimetres of brain damage.

Although it was thought that he would have problems in walking, he proved everyone wrong by walking before starting school. The use of only his right hand was frustrating for him, but as with everything in his life, Lee persevered and found ways to do things with one hand, constantly shunning attempts from people who tried to help. Things were difficult – doctors' visits, hospital appointments, numerous experts, all with mind-boggling information about the condition and its cause, yet unfortunately there was no cure. He was taken to countless specialists who all confirmed that the only improvements that could be made in his condition would be the improvements that he himself made. It became clear that if nothing was done to help him with this, his condition would deteriorate. So, with endless exercise programmes obtained from professionals, Lee was thrown into a battle of making his arm and leg move by sheer willpower, as the part of his brain that automatically told his left arm and leg what to do was too damaged to do its job. Progress was very gradual, with no overnight improvements, and every minute step forward required huge effort and application.

At five years old Lee attended Barton Clough Primary School in Manchester, a mainstream school, although he could have been placed in a special school. After being assessed it was decided that he would be better suited to a mainstream environment due to the fact his disability was purely physical.

When Lee turned eight, he and his four-year-old brother were taken from Manchester by their mother to live in Scotland. With the support of Women's Aid, and with just the clothes they were wearing, they fled their home due to domestic violence. Following five months in a refuge, Lee, his mother and brother were allocated a house on the outskirts of Edinburgh, where they began a new life – using an assumed name for their safety.

During his primary school years, Lee made friends but sadly also suffered the inevitable taunts regarding his impairment. As time went on, he became more and more withdrawn as children made his life a misery. Unable to stand up for himself or fight back, he relied on his younger brother to deal with things for him. Both brothers were very keen on football, and played and watched it regularly. Football was later to become the one and only solid comfort in Lee's life.

Come the age of twelve, Lee, his brother, mother and her new partner moved to the Scottish Borders. Before beginning the term at the local High School, a meeting took place to explain to the school that due to his physical state Lee had endured endless bullying, destroying his confidence and making his life unbearable. Given hope of a better future and feeling more secure, Lee settled into the life of a new town and education system.

Sadly, this time of relative calm did not last for long, as quite rapidly the discrimination and intimidation began again, with the aggression shown from children a lot older building up quickly, resulting in Lee sinking into a deeper depression. Attending school only under duress, Lee spent most of his spare time in his bedroom listening to music and playing on the computer, thus isolating himself from family and friends. His attitude to life became filled with hopelessness, and on retreating even further into despair Lee attempted suicide. This cry for help resulted in his being sent over a lengthy period of time to a variety of counselling organisations. Each tried hard, but without success, to break down the wall that he had had to build up over the years in order to survive. Everyone owed Lee a favour. He hadn't asked for the hand he'd been dealt, and although he realised that there were a lot of people worse off than he was, life was demonstrably very hard for him.

Football continued to play a big part in Lee's life – his two teams being Manchester City and Aberdeen. As a result of not getting to as many matches as he wanted, Lee wrote football articles for local junior and senior sides and had them published week after week – something he was good at and received praise for.

At the age of nineteen, Lee decided it was time to try 'independent living'. He moved out of what had been his home of several years, leaving his mother, her partner and two younger brothers. His flat was just a mile away, but Lee could enjoy the solitude and freedom from restrictions. He could come and go as he pleased, eventually venturing into the local social scene. Regrettably, events of taunting on an adult level multiplied, but Lee did not let this pattern drive him back into isolation.

Eight years on, Lee still lives on his own and has a small circle of friends, yet experiences daily abuse concerning his disability and being spoken to like a second-rate citizen. Most of the time Lee tries not to let it bother him, but on occasion the torment becomes excruciating, and once again he seeks haven in his own universe where no one can reach him.

It was during one of these spells that Lee began to write his short stories. He could stay in, sitting in front of his laptop and pouring out his thoughts and innermost feelings in a clear, coherent style. His vivid imagination and grasp of the English language enable Lee to live through his writings much of what he is unable to express by other means.

Family and friends love him dearly, and to his mother he will always be her very special first-born son.

Gina

Life's a Gamble

I think I will put twenty on Galantos at Kempton. But having decided this, I didn't fancy losing that much on one donkey. Mm... Could cover myself and do it each way. Then again, whatever happened to living life for the moment without regrets? Folk say it's a mug's game. Come on, I do need a vice of sorts. Don't drink, don't smoke or do drugs... What can I do? Huh! Can you imagine one of Adam Ant's biggest hits as my signature tune. Nah, don't even go there!

'Right, Kath, I'll take that.'

'You feeling all right son? You never usually stick this much on.'

'I know, but I'm having one of my crazy days. I'm in a silly mood. I wouldn't be human if I didn't go nuts once in a while.'

'True, son. Wouldn't have you any other way.'

'Just noticed whilst looking at the betting, Kath... I've taken 3/1 on Galantos when it's actually 8/1.'

'Well, what you want to do? I can't give you your money back. Slip's gone through the till.'

'Don't fancy losing twenty on an 8/1 shot.'

'Can have a tenner each way at eights, or change the horse completely.'

'Tell you what, Kath... Seeing as I've written 3/1, put it on the favourite. Yeah?'

'Okay, son.'

That's when the trouble all started. A furlong out, it looked as though my luck for the week was changing. Olivino, the favourite, was seemingly pissing the race, only for Galantos somewhere out of the picture to come rattling home to win by five lengths.

I was beginning to question my whole life. All my days, I'd gone against my gut instinct and had failed miserably. Was that my lesson before I left to join the other side – to have a bit more faith in my convictions? How was I ever going to move forward in this world if I didn't test my limits? It wasn't so much that I'd missed out on a hundred and sixty quid, but more that I'd changed my mind.

To learn anything from this experience, I had to realise that it was I who was to shoulder the blame for this downfall, and nobody else. Was it because no one expected me to achieve anything in life? So, what was I to do with myself? Any aspirations that I had meant nothing, if not a soul showed interest or a passion for what I was trying to accomplish. As it was, I had gone a bit daft and had twenty on the next donkey derby without success. The thing was that I didn't actually have twenty on me to give Kath, so to compensate I stuck thirty on the next race, hoping I wouldn't need to owe her fifty the following day.

Yep, you guessed it. I lost again. I was now starting to lose the plot, and with two contests still to go before the end of the evening, the red mist took control even further. Another fifty down the pan... So, Robert would be pleasantly surprised when I went in to hand over a hundred notes – which I wouldn't normally have spent, if I hadn't had such a big overdraft agreement. I cut myself some slack and put the debacle down to sheer bad luck. These kinds of things were sent to test us. Eh?

I know this is going to sound like a strange time to bring it up, but I've never been in love. Don't get me wrong. I've fancied lots of women. However, because the attraction hasn't been mutual, I've quite easily disregarded what I felt. There are women who are still quite old-fashioned, and like a man to do the chasing. I'm taking the fact that no woman has ever made the first move as a sign that no female has ever seen me as the perfect catch.

I know that sometimes I can be a bit of an idiot, but I think that half the time it's because I'm trying to keep my cool so that others don't know how unhappy I am. I mean, if they don't know anything's wrong, then they can't help. Right?

It's something I've felt since I was a young boy – not being understood. Yes, we are all unique, but not all of us are 'different'. Many choose to be part of the flock – afraid to stand out from the crowd, in fear of rejection. I'm okay. I've already had my biggest knock-back – the absence of my father. Nearly twenty years ago now. It's not a unique situation in today's society, I know, but the hurt never goes away. To not see the man who in one way or another gave you life, is a tough nut to crack. I suppose it's his loss, though. If I look back, I can see that he's missed out on a great deal during all the time he's been absent.

Still doesn't make it right, though.

The thing that baffles me is that for almost two decades we've been less than five hours from each other in a car. Our lives could have crossed so many times and we would never have known it. Despite everything, I think about him most days, hoping that he's okay and having a good life. He might not deserve my concern, but everyone should get a second chance. I'm not one for holding grudges. Guess I'm maturing quicker than I thought. It was different when I was a kid, but as I've got older I've learned that all the pent-up anger ain't worth it. Better put to use in a more constructive manner. Can't let this beat me for the rest of my life, can I? I don't feel sorry for him or anything. He's just a person in the past who has taught me a lot of lessons about how not to treat people, especially women.

Doing more than just surviving today. Living life to the max is pretty awesome! This is why I'm about to meet up with a woman I've known for years, to have some fun. Yes, no strings sex. How good does that sound? Especially because she's paying for my body...

We first met not long after I moved into my own flat. Nothing stunning. I can see that she's not even my soulmate, which is why I can separate love from a 'shag'.

Don't particularly want to settle down with anyone right now. I'm too independent for all that palava at my age. Want to go and see the planet on which I live before getting a mortgage and kids, if that's what I fancy at all.

If she's daft enough to give me money for my 'excellent services', who am I to argue, and so spoil another's happiness? I'll never pester her for the dough. I don't even set a price. She just gives it to me when she can. Assesses my performance, then decides on a figure. Okay, I'm not making my millions yet. Might be selling myself short, but I've always done what I've had to do to survive.

Tell you what's made a massive difference. Coming off my epilepsy tablets. I'm not any less emotional. I'm just able to manage my feelings a lot better. Never did I think I'd ever find myself in this position. This is why life and its unpredictability are worth the hassle every time. If anyone found out, I don't think that I could handle the small-mindedness. People have the knack of poking their noses into matters that don't concern them.

The reason why I go and see her on my terms is that I don't want to attract suspicion to my activities. It's not that I've anything to hide. It's just that I like to keep my private life exactly that: private. Nobody's getting hurt, so what's the problem? Women have been prostituting themselves for centuries. There are lots of blokes who are now male escorts, and that's widely accepted as normal practice. Women can find it just as hard to find suitable company as us men.

Bit of a laugh in all honesty – doing things I never thought I would. Role-playing and a whiff of sadomasochism didn't do anyone any harm, did it? All a learning curve – taking into account another's needs and wants. It's something I ain't done a lot of in the past. Never had to.

I've only ever been intimate with one before her. When it came to that relationship, I was too young and immature to hold down a commitment as big as the one she wanted from me. Not that I didn't want it. But I was affected by my mother's two failed marriages. I wasn't even eighteen when she got divorced for the second time! Hopefully it'll be third time lucky. Has been seven years now, so let's pray they don't go through 'the itch'.

Did I have the tools to make a go of the good, the bad and the ugly, which comes with every romance? I've never felt I have. I'm kind of fussy regarding women, though you wouldn't think so from what I've just told you. Refuse to settle for second best, and would rather be on my own. But I'll never say 'never'. That's like saying that you can't be blessed – which ain't my experience.

If you believe what my grandmother says, I've been touched by the hand of God. I've suffered (if you can call it that) from hemiplegia since birth. It's a form of cerebal palsy that affects one side of the body. My family were told I'd never walk, play for Manchester United or be a concert pianist. First of all it'd be a cardinal sin to change my allegiance to the red side of the city, considering I've been a blue all my life! And secondly, I'm more of a drumming fan than a keys man. I defied the critics, and walked before I started school. Granted, I may go about my business on the left toes and right heel – though surely, if that's the only hindrance I've to put up with, I'll be doing fine. That, and a left arm which has a mind of it's own. You should see it when it gets an idea into its head! It's unstoppable. Really is an experience to witness it in action.

Well, the explanation for my miraculous partial recovery is a trip to

4

Lourdes that I was taken on when eighteen months old. Maybe now, as a guy in his twenties, they'd like to take me back and get a head transplant.

Whilst I was on this sabbatical, my father was elsewhere. So it was left to them, Grandma and Uncle Chris, to accompany me on this last-chance-saloon pilgrimage. Of course, I wasn't old enough to remember any of it, though, from what I was told, a small, scruffy, smelly-looking man approached Uncle Chris in the hotel bar. He asked to be shown to the room where the sick baby boy was. How did he know what sex I was for a start? And why out of all the people in the bar did he choose Uncle Chris? A little reluctant to have anything to do with this apparent charlatan, Uncle Chris agreed to his pleas with some scepticism. The weird thing was that 'the vision of Jesus', as Grandma puts it, never introduced himself. While my grandma, who was sitting on the end of the bed, cradled me, he massaged his healing hands all over my skin. Then, as he opened the door, he turned and said: 'Take him to the grotto tomorrow, and splash the holy water in the sign of the cross over his forehead.'

My grandfather is a non-believer at the best of times, and he wanted to get to the bottom of this encounter with the mystery man, and so he gave a description to staff members in the hotel. The lady behind the desk at reception said that they were unable to help. Seemingly, nobody with such appalling body odour would ever have been allowed to check in.

After the initial meeting, the family never saw this individual again. It was as though he had literally disappeared into thin air without trace. However, they did as the stranger had asked, and within three weeks of returning home, hey presto, I was walking!

When Grandma had enthralled me with the fable I told her to politely: 'Eff off, Gran. I'm not so special that Jesus in the disguise of a small, scruffy, smelly-looking man would come to earth and weave his spiritual powers of curing on me.'

Needless to say, she gave me a telling off for speaking to my elders with such disrespect. So I don't know what people were worried about.

Not long into the agreement with my female 'client', she kept making excuses as to why she couldn't pay me. At first it didn't bother me, as long as I got it eventually. I'm not the type to put fear into the eyes of anybody who breaks a promise. I just don't appreciate people who say they're going to do something but then at the last minute let you down. You do get the people who have the best intentions in the world, yet have terrible punctuality. In all fairness, I kind of thought something like this would happen. I suppose that when you get into a situation and it's going tits up, there's always the potential for fireworks. Although I didn't want to let rip, I felt I had to. I mean, nothing is ever free in life anymore, so why should I sit there and take the new climate as it stood? Nobody is thick enough to work and not get paid. Well, at least I'm not. People moan when I say I'm on benefits. Then, if I do get an offer of work, I turn it down so folk don't moan because I'm not declaring it to 'the social'. But why should I turn something down, if it's only a one off? Surely people realise that if it was a regular income on a more permanent basis, I'd stand up and be counted. That's right... others don't see it like that. Never will. I can't bloody win! Okay, my way of earning a little extra cash has to be considered carefully – unless, of course, the money is really a series of gifts.

What goes on between two consenting adults behind closed doors should remain behind closed doors. Got nothing to do with anybody else. I usually find that people who want to know the gory details of your life don't have a life of their own to see to.

Maybe I should take up a proposition that had been made to me, and venture into the unknown for a better existence. Bernie, a workie I met in the pub, had offered me two hundred pounds cash in hand, plus travelling expenses, to wherever I wanted to go to never set foot in Duns again. In a heated conversation, he told me that for one so bright I didn't show it, and as long as I stayed here I'd die a slow death. The people who could help me achieve my ambitions of writing for TV, radio, theatre and for the papers just weren't in town. For the necessary support I would have to leave to locate these saviours. The catch in his proposal was that I had to go without telling a soul. Couldn't do that to my mother. She's the only one who knows and understands why I am the way I am, having going through all the hardship with me. His deal was that I should show up on site to collect the money, and then away I would go to find the life I craved.

I have to say that it was kind of tempting to go, and leave all the shit behind. I wouldn't miss it, especially seeing as though I had nothing to stay for. The quiz hadn't been the same since the team fell one by one like soldiers in the heat of battle, while at the darts I never played like I knew I could in practice, so was no good to anyone – not even myself. Having no job meant no notice to hand in, and no girlfriend/wife and kids to consider made the decision even simpler. The world was my oyster.

However, something was holding me back. I had unfinished business in many areas of my life. The lifeline that Bernie was throwing would always remain on the table, but I would need to get a lot of things signed, sealed and delivered before I went. But why I just couldn't go, and keep my silence, was beyond anyone's wildest imagination. Was it because I was sick of running away? And sick of not letting people know how I really felt? You know, wanting to smack a certain somebody before leaving – to unleash so many torturous memories from down the years. Why do you think I'd done nothing yet? *Because most weren't worth wasting my time and effort on.*

Actually, I'm waiting on Karma to play its hand and even things out. I really do believe life has a way of the good prevailing over evil in the long term. When it came to friends, I could count them on one hand, and I had lost the closeness with nearly every one of them. Joe and Ed were too busy with their own lives to know what I was up to, while Rich and Lisa were just as crap at keeping in touch. Then, when it came to Kirsten and Meg, they'd like to know who my client was rather than why I was doing it in the first place, so what was the point in our friendships?

If my mate came up to me and said: 'How would you feel if I told you I was selling my body?' the first question wouldn't be: 'Who is it?' Instead, it would most probably be: 'Why are you disrespecting yourself like that?' – or words to that effect.

After discussing Bernie's olive branch with various confidantes, I decided to choose life as opposed to an early grave. The only person other than my mum who I wanted to know what I was doing was the girl who had been my first love. It was just a pity that she wasn't going on the exciting adventure with me. I missed her so much. Funny how you only ever miss something once it's gone. Even though we'd never slept together or seen one another for over five years, we'd always said, 'No matter what happens between us we'll forever remain friends.' I'm glad to say that the promise has been kept. I didn't want to part, though. Maybe it was fate's way of telling me that she was someone I had to let go of before I could realise how much she thought of me. Took the girl about two years to get over our break-up. Surely I'm not that special, or maybe I am and just didn't know it. She nearly got married a few years back, and wanted me there – which would have killed me inside – but as long as she was happy, who was I to put a spanner in the works? Mum reckons that we might get back together later in life. However, she's already said that she won't have me back to suffer the heartache again. We'd obviously be different people, after all the time spent at opposite ends of the country, but I don't see a problem. It's so unfair. Matters were taken out of my control.

I don't take too kindly to people sorting out their issues through violence. I'm not going into the ins and outs of it, but to be threatened, without being given the benefit of the doubt, is pretty devastating. To let an outsider destroy what was a perfectly good relationship, despite not meeting me face-to-face, looms on the brink of obsession. With their insecurities, those concerned can't have made many mates along the way. I'm very proud of where I come from and won't change for anybody. Though I'd never go back to Manchester, I think I speak for most of my hommies when I say 'what you see is what you get, so either like or lump me'. And I'd add: 'It's your choice. I'm not going to lose sleep over the ignorance.'

I'm the first to admit that I'm probably the biggest waster of all time. Now, if it's possible, I'd like to compare myself with some of my fellow Mancs. Yep, Ian, John, Mani and Reni – known as The Stone Roses – in the eyes of many could have ruled the world if they'd wanted. The thing was, they actually did. It's just that folk didn't know it. Pulled off all they set out to do and more. And on drugs... How impressive! Weren't on the planet to satisfy anyone else. It was once reported that they went into the studio for a ten-hour session, but did just one track. It really took all of ten minutes, since they were so 'off their faces'. They played hard as well as worked hard, and that's probably why there was five years between records. They were very meticulous in their goal to never sound like anyone before them. Ian once said of Mani and Reni: 'They were the best rhythm section to come out of the UK.'

That's the reason that I bring the band up. Quiet confidence is often mistaken for arrogance. Yet that never bothered them. There are so many people trying to drag you down that it's a wonder anybody gets anywhere on the scene. It's no surprise then that they're widely regarded as one of British music's top underachievers. A bit like myself, eh? Loads of potential, and never realising just how much talent I'm actually throwing away. This puts me in the category of the many masterminds, who through their own thought process become Japanese kamikaze-style fighter pilots. Using and abusing a gift is the sign of a troubled character unaware of how to blossom. Almost as if we say to ourselves 'it's ours, and we'll only share it with the world if we want to'.

In my case, I believe it's because everything I've done writing-wise is largely underappreciated. Take my football reports as an example. I rarely got my name printed, and even when I did, it was never my own. I'll always remember one report I did, describing a goal that we scored at Edinburgh City. Referred to Phil and Jimmy as 'the headless chicken and vulture' striking partnership. Now, I thought that this was a great way of showing they complemented each other – one, a tireless player doing all the hard graft, and the other, his mate, the glory hunter, feeding off scraps. I was not the Sports Editor at the paper. Hence, I left my post of press correspondent shortly after. That's why, if I can influence just one part of my life, then let it be my funeral.

Chances are that I might not come back from my trip round the globe. What I will say is that if you can't picture me dancing to the song I'm about to reveal, then it's clear to me that you never really knew who I was. Just make sure you get the nine minute fifty-three second version of the track to those who turn up. It'll be interesting to see who makes an effort. I'll never forget the way I was left in the lurch for my 26th birthday – though we'll not get into that here, because there's a time and a place. Can see the vicar now: 'Lee's requested we play the Stone Roses and their infectious hit FOOL'S GOLD!'

Okay, I've still got a few more years left in me yet, though this life malarkey puzzles me. Why go through all the things we enjoy and despise, only to end up six feet under? What's the point of us being here, only to become lost in nothingness, where nobody has recollection of who we were?

Turning to my father one last time. He really has made me the man I am today. I decided not to follow his example, because I'm better than that and want more for myself. Yes, I have my moments, but doesn't everybody? Maybe different surroundings might inspire my best material. I just don't know. Put it this way, Duns has provided lots of tales, and I probably need to get away before the juices will start to flow. As for the unfinished business I talked about... Seems that I really didn't have any after all. The people I cared for weren't who I thought they were. Time to go and see Bernie. He'll be in the Swan.

Fascinating concept – a gambling addiction leading to someone being a sex maniac, isn't it? One feeds the other, and vice versa, eh? Scary to think I got through it without support from family, friends or the professional sector. It's true what they say. You're born on your own, and you die on your own. Yes, a problem shared is a problem halved, but that's it. Was my problem that fact that I had to work through it alone? I did some lying along the way, although nothing which should upset anybody. Made of sterner stuff – so my sex therapist, Irina Myskow, said. After three appointments, she claimed she couldn't help because I didn't have a proper relationship with a lover. If I was able to 'get it up for my "client"', then physically there was no need to be seeing a therapist. I'd have liked to attend Gamblers Anonymous if my doctor had made plans to be spoken to. Why, if it's anonymous, do we stand up and say: 'Hello, I'm Lee, and I'm addicted to gambling?'

Kept myself busy during the day – to take away the temptation of walking into the shop. Relapsed a few times, and when back on the wagon for good, I realised that there are better things to spend my money on. I was a single bloke with nothing going on – no fulfilment... nothing. Fancied living abroad ever since I was a kid. Informed Mum at eight years old that I was marrying an Ulrika Jonsson lookalike when I was older. That's when the charm with Sweden and its Scandinavian counterparts began. Love how the country maintains its mediaeval feel, yet still moves with the modern times. What will I do when I get there? Visit the Ullevi Stadium, site of Aberdeen's greatest ever footballing night. And that's just for starters. But if I'm being honest, I don't really know. We'll see once I've touched down. It's half the fun. Göteborg, here we come!

Diamond is a Man's Best Friend

They say that you only leave this planet once you've learned all your lessons. Now, I'm no religious zombie, but I must have a few more to go as I'm still here! The story I'm about to tell is one actually based on real life. Yes, it really happened to yours truly.

I'd been in a rut for some time, and desperately needed to be out of my current situation, which was just dozing about, going nowhere in particular. All my mates had fled the small town mentality that had surrounded us as we grew up together. I only had my mother and youngest brother to worry about. Talking to the same people, and about the same things, day after day, night after night, week after week, saw me lose the will to live. I'd already tried to kill myself six times. What more did I have to do to make people sit up and take notice of my plight? Some might argue that the development of an addiction to gambling was inevitable. I'd frequently begun to switch off from everything around me, and nobody had picked up on it.

Everyone's feelings and opinions should count for something. Not mine. Apparently I'd exaggerated the many thoughts in my head, leading most to dismiss them. How another can tell you how to feel is beyond me. What bothers one might not necessarily bother another. Consideration for others has never been a strong point of us humans, has it? It's a dog-eat-dog world, no matter who tries to convince me otherwise.

Well, this one morning, I decided to take a trip to the city. Retail therapy was the plan of action to take away the blues. My woes would still be waiting for me when I got back, but I was doing this just now for my own sanity. I couldn't remember the last time someone did anything nice for me. Why not? I always try to look after Number One. If you don't, nobody ever will. Whenever you get the chance, spoil yourself. I wasn't sure if those around me understood what made me tick. Would they ever? That's right... I had to open up more first. What was the point? They never listened. Everyone seemed to know what was best

11

for me, before I knew myself.

On the afternoon that ultimately changed my life for good, I'd arranged to meet my other brother for lunch. I was in no hurry, so stood on Princes Street, waiting to cross one of the side alleys at a set of lights. The sudden sight of beautiful girl took my breath away. She was the kind that makes a mockery of love at first sight. Beauty is in the eye of the beholder.

So, for anyone tuning in, I want you to picture what you think she might look like. I've got to keep a little bit for myself, right? There were never any like her back home, nor would you expect to find one. Made me realise what I'd missed out on all these years. No way on God's green earth was she single. The so-called good ones were always taken, and whoever the other was, he was a lucky bloke. I had to stop fantasising, or else I would be heading for a direct collision course with this stranger. The longer the lights took to change, the closer she was getting and the more nervous I was becoming. Having said that, maybe accidentally bumping into her, so that the pile of books she was carrying would fall, might not be such a bad way of breaking the ice. After all, why wasn't I deserving of such a gorgeous creature? Okay, there was no guarantee that she had the brains to go with the looks, but was I forever going to play the hard luck card, or would I bite the bullet and somehow ask her out? There were only two answers she could give.

Of course, there were plenty more fish in the sea if I got knocked back. I had to take a risk – something I'd not really done throughout my life. Yet I did nothing. Never been great at selling myself, and I felt maybe the opportunity to change that had now gone. Many I know for a bet would ask her out, despite knowing that she might be the high-maintenance type, who would eventually ditch them anyway – for being too nice a fella – and go with the proverbial 'bad boy'.

That's what I'd never understood about women. These rogues break their heart, and yet in all honesty they're the ones to blame for trying to change their men. I've no sympathy, because they can't have it both ways. They make their beds, and should learn to lie in them. If you want to be with me you've got to be committed one hundred and ten per cent, and not feel as though you're settling for second best, just because the desired prize has eff-ed up again! I can always be nasty in the bedroom and a gentleman outside it. If that's what they want, it's not a problem. Sadly, I'm not a mind reader, and so I need to be told these things!

The infatuation with this lady deepened even further after I overheard one sentence of the conversation she was having on her mobile. I'll remember the words forever: 'Look, I'm not saying I don't want to see you again.'

I'd become part of her life without even trying. Why was it that I'd zoned in on this private discussion, and not the barny a middle-aged couple were having while standing next to me at the lights, or perhaps the spectacular scenery Scotland's capital had to offer? I really can't answer that one.

Until I met my brother that line messed with my mind. Who was she talking to? I needed to find out, yet it was none of my business. She could have been talking about a number of things. Was she letting someone down after a disastrous blind date – the one a friend has organised to get you over that serious long-term relationship which didn't end in a fairytale wedding liked you hoped, but was a complete and utter waste of time? Or was it a date which she was afraid to turn down, knowing it'd be the best offer of a 'shag' she'd had as a singleton? (Especially seeing how the opposite sex had detected that she was desperate to keep in tow with all her friends who were happily settled in their relationships?) We've all been there. Don't say you haven't, or you're a liar. Anything to appear normal in today's society, eh?

I hid the intrigue from my brother, Paul, as I only intended to stay for a few hours before catching the train home. Little did I know that accepting an invite to a stag night would alter my slant on women completely. I hate the word 'fate'.

They say that you can always tell when you've met 'the one' – or so folk keep telling me. One thing's for sure, I didn't think I'd ever meet that girl again. Paul's crowd decided to gatecrash one of the city's classier strip joints. I'd never been in one of these establishments – so had never lived until then. You had the choice of whatever lass you wanted, as long as you could afford her and didn't expect a sexual service. There was one on the main stage who I thought I recognised as the chick from earlier in the day. I knew for definite it was she when she tapped me on the shoulder to get my attention. Boy, did she get my undivided attention! She was even more stunning in her skimpy wee outfit – which showed off her perfectly-toned body. It was as though I'd died and gone to heaven as she teased me to go somewhere a little more

13

private with her erotic dance on my lap.

'Diamond', as she was called, had clocked me coming in, and knew that she'd bumped into the same guy who had been acting strangely at the lights on her lunch break. But what she didn't let on was that she knew that this geezer had been admiring her from afar – hence the reason she hadn't freaked out.

Was it possible that I'd been on her mind just as much as she'd been on mine? Somehow she had known that I wasn't some sad punter she looked upon as she did most of the other sleazy customers. I was different, having never before been in one of these parlours – which degrade women, and exploit the men that go there. Despite what I've said, the female species has always captivated me. Although we both knew that we were breaking club policies, not even the see-through window, or interference from Diamond's bodyguard, could prevent us from having the most wonderful sex I ever imagined. It was my first time, and to say that she made me feel special, and not perverted, is an understatement. I think that Vernon (who was built like a brick 'shit house') accepted that our attraction was for real, and so left us to talk into the small hours.

The guy she'd been speaking to was a regular client of hers called Brian, who couldn't take no for an answer. He wanted Diamond, or Sarah as he preferred to call her, to move in with him. The catch was that he was married with three grown-up children, and was prepared to leave his wife, Marion, for her. Once realising he'd taken it too far, he backed down and agreed to give the best part of forty-two years another go. As for me, I bagged the elusive mobile number and started dating the girl.

We lasted just seven months, in which I learned a lot about myself. Broke up because I couldn't handle other men ogling over the woman I had fallen head over heels in love with. She needed the money to pay for her last year at university – so I was right, the woman did have some intellect. She had never taken a penny from a man before and wasn't starting now – which I respected.

The moral of this tale? There are many. Firstly, unless you ask, you'll never know. I mean I never thought she'd look twice at me. Not all the ladies are superficial. The rugged sporty type or the muscular Greek Adonis sort only get so far. We only think they want these fakes. Instead, most are probably searching for something much deeper. We

14

mere mortals think we're out of their league. That's only because some put us out of their league. Nobody should ever be out of anyone's league. Unfortunately the world doesn't work like that. All they want is for someone to wine and dine them. Not to mention providing a kiss and a cuddle now and then. Suppose it's not too much to ask for from us blokes, is it?

My own most personal lesson? If one who is called 'good looking' can accept me as I am physically, then surely I can accept myself too? I've not seen Sarah for months now. Hopefully one day, once the dust has had time to settle, we can meet up and joke about how we met twice in the same day. In a funny kind of way, she saved my life and highlighted just how much more living I've still to do.

So, in summary, people hear me when I say that if I can change, so can you. How come? Simple really. Diamond Is A Man's Best Friend!

Suisexual

'We only get one shot at this life – it ain't a dress rehearsal,' I told my mate, Dave. Nearly four years on, it was plain to see that this piece of advice had gone in one ear and out of the other.

As a man who's not offended by anything whatsoever, I wasn't the least bit surprised when Dave revealed that he'd fancied me for months, wanted to jump on me for weeks and even had a couple of wet dreams about me. Most sex-crazy males of my age would have run in the opposite direction as fast and as far away as possible. Not me. I decided to help him to see that he could, if he so wished, live the life he so richly deserved. First, he had to stop living a lie and be proud of who he really was – either that, or remain unhappy till the day he died. The tragic thing was that he'd already wasted thirty plus years trying to be normal and fit in. He certainly needed the encouragement to get the best out of what life he had left.

Everybody, in one way or another, is scared of change, especially if people are set in their particular fashions. At the end of the day, only he could determine if the gamble was worth taking. Those around him could only be there for the geezer in the commitment made.

Yes, I'm flattered by the fact that Dave looked on me in that manner, though he knows I can't return the feeling. I've had first-hand experience of unrequited love, and it's one of the worst aspects of life as an adult. I really can't explain how I get myself into these situations, but wouldn't have it any other way!

Fate is a strange concept, and I believe that everything happens for a reason. How much we have a say in how our life pans out, I'm not quite sure – not a great deal, I think. If we delve into the whole holy argument, travelling down that road might suggest that Dave will receive a hot reception in hell – what with homosexuality being something which the people who practise the Christian faith frown upon. Does anybody really believe this outdated nonsense? Next, you'll be telling me that people will, if they aren't careful, be asphyxiated into submission for not abiding to the powers above.

Is devotion to a religion's beliefs not an individual's failure to find fulfilment? Allowing ourselves to become brainwashed into thinking that certain things are what really happen when we peg it is rather barmy. Is not half the excitement about where we go the surprise that tests us when we get there? Surely can't be any worse than the environment we live in at the present moment. However, until our number's up we should try and relish the gateway we've been given as much as possible.

Hence, I think about the time when Dave tried to commit hara-kiri. You're a fool if you think it was just work that almost tipped a troubled soul over the edge. It's a night I'll remember for a very long time – seeing a mate in such a bloody mess. This cry for help made me ponder about whether or not I had been the best a friend could be. The signs had been there, but I had just decided to ignore them, instead preferring to listen to the idle gossip that declared he was an attention-seeking crackpot who'd pulled this stunt many times before. I hope if any of these people find themselves in the same position there's not as much apathy towards them as there was towards Dave – and that perhaps would make the difference between life and death.

I only stumbled across the rubble whilst walking home from the pub and hearing a commotion bellowing out of the bedroom window. Rushing to the rescue, I thought I might have to break down the front door, though managed to slip in the back via the communal garden. Faced with an illuminated, loud, deserted living room, it didn't give away any clues as to the mayhem upstairs. There I was confronted by one of the most gruesome sights I've ever witnessed. There was blood everywhere – on the carpet, staining the mattress, and smeared in Dave's clothes. I felt as if I were in my own horror movie – and it challenged what nerve I possessed.

Knowing that the half-dressed Dave was in no immediate danger – having cut across the wrist with a potato peeler, as opposed to down the vein for maximum effect – I focussed on reassuring him that everything was going to be okay, while waiting for the ambulance to arrive to patch him up.

I'm actually quite proud of myself for the way I conducted things at the hospital. I appreciate that not everyone in a crisis can react in the best possible way. How I ever got through the episode intact, I'll never know. I was so angry at his brother about not calling for medical assistance.

Before I arrived, Dave had refused to bring attention to himself, pleading to let everything just carry on the next day as if nothing had happened. Did he think people wouldn't start asking questions when they saw the state of his wrists? And as for his youngest sibling... if Dave told him to jump off a cliff would he do it? Evidently he had no savvy to realise Dave wasn't in the right frame of mind to be making decisions for himself at a time like that. The fella needed some TLC to face his demons – care which regrettably didn't materialize. Could things get worse? I had wondered. But then they got even more chronic as his brother asked me what to say to the operator when phoning for an ambulance!

'Tell them he's won the eff-ing lottery! What do you think you tell them?' The words screamed silently in my head.

As Dave was lifted into the back of the ambulance, one of the paramedics told me to fill an overnight bag with at least one clean outfit.

What I wasn't expecting was to be joining Dave as his moral support. The lone thing that sticks in my mind about those seven or so hours was the people that worked in the A&E department. There was a mean-looking security man who nipped out for a cigarette at every given opportunity, and a shy cleaner who was sweeping the same part of the floor over and over again, making me feel dizzy. And as for the mail boy... by the time dawn cracked he'd have walked a marathon twice! The mixed breed of consultants didn't save too many lives, with us being two of only four people in the waiting room throughout the duration. I saw a lot of hilarity in the nurse station. Now I come to think of it, the girls at reception did nothing but read magazines until needing to pick up the phone. Okay, through the week they'll experience quiet shifts, I decided. That morning, when I trotted round the perimeter of the hospital grounds, the only excitement generated was my presence scaring fellow colleagues with my shadow, as if some kind of weird intruder. Just went for a breather to take everything in.

Found a note in Dave's trouser pocket, citing his resignation from an organisation I thought might have been important to him. I had been told to look for clues as to why he would take great lengths to end his own life, as he'd distressed himself that much he was being sick every two or three minutes and couldn't speak. At four in the morning, the head of the unit said that we were ready to vacate the bed space, but because I couldn't contact my mum, and Dave refused to disturb family at unsociable hours, we had to wait for the twenty to seven bus to Duns. Mum would have collected us had I been able to explain the position I was in. All part of the adventure – taking an hour's ride by public transport! Flicking through glossy women's supplements until the single decker machine drove in was not my idea of bridging the gap.

Having not prepared a packed lunch for an incident like this, I became rather peckish. But as the canteen was shut, I resigned myself to the fact that a very small cup of tea from the lady behind the desk was the best offer of refreshment I was going to get.

To give Dave his due, he paid my share of the fare because I'd only gone out with a few quid in my slacks and left the free bus pass at the flat! It was pretty surreal – with us being the only passengers for a driver who took a detour and stopped in the middle of nowhere between Earlston and Gordon to deliver a jar of coffee to the front porch of a farmhouse.

After jumping from the bus, I tucked Dave into bed as if we'd never set foot out of the door, and then headed to my mum's for a little comfort in a bowl of cereal. This was something I'd not done since leaving the school nine years previously. Seeing the world first thing – when normal folk go about their business – was an amazing discovery.

Dave was referred to a counsellor, where he seems to have dealt with whatever was bothering him, and he now has a new job that he appears to enjoy. Be warned readers, if he ever tries to pull another trick like the one that evening, I make no bones about it by saying that I'll finish the job on his behalf once and for all. So the Danny La Rue I know survives to fight another day.

One last thing. There's a notion that everyone needs a gay friend. I've got mine. Have you got yours?

Burning Desire

'You miserable bastards, you miserable fucking bastards!'

It only took a few seconds to flee the battlefield and find cover in the toilets. I'd been wounded in more ways than one, and so I needed a plan. Allowing myself to play the part of a Iraqi suicide bomber wasn't an option. The time had come to stop justifying my existence. For twenty-five years people seemed to think that I owed them something. I didn't, though. I owed to myself to enjoy life to the max. Probably the reason why I was unhappy was that I listened to folk too much. Never going to go anywhere or achieve anything if I didn't alter things. Maybe it was my fault for not making a stand at school. You know, if I'm seen as an easy target, then it's no wonder they keep trying to get a reaction. No resistance meant more fun for them. However, to set fire to someone's personal property is beyond a joke. Mum's going to kill me. I'm not condoning what they've done. To do it once might be a laugh, although twice is a bit sadistic. Terrorists – that's what they are, though on a smaller scale.

It's all very well saying that the hat was an embarrassment, but wasn't that for me to decide? I mean, who made them style critics? Whatever happened to man being able to have freedom of choice? I've never intentionally offended or even hurt anyone, so how are they getting away with it? How would they like it if I did something similar to them? They would be just as furious as I am now. But I've not got a bad bone in my body to inflict such torture on anyone.

The thing that's got my back up is that everybody just stood there as though it was normal behaviour. I certainly know who my friends are now, or who they aren't. What was I supposed to do? Challenge him in a crowded pub with the hat alight? Don't be silly, it could have started a bigger blaze. Seeing him parade the hat was like watching an executioner, seconds after he'd decapitated his subject. It's something I'll never forget till the day I die.

Wish there was something I could do which they'd never forget –

except it would have to be something that was not as satanic. I know. How about taking my own life? Maybe walk in front of a car on the way home. Nah, that's too unoriginal. How about I get Rab and the boys down from Uddingston to teach them a lesson. They always said they'd lend a hand if I was ever facing difficulties. They knew how the locals made my life a misery for no apparent reason. But I'd only be stooping to their level if I did. I would still like to see them, though. It's been four years since they left the place. Then again, I don't know what the natives of this town are capable of, so to start a mini-war is kind of naïve. The repercussions of such retribution are potentially fatal. Are people like that worth it? In a word, no. I'll let the big man upstairs name their fate. It's a pity that it could take a while, though. As long as I'm there to see it, I suppose it doesn't matter how long it takes. Police would just laugh in my face too. And even if they did take me seriously, I would probably just create more enemies for myself – which round here isn't the sort of thing you want to do. It's not a good idea to alienate yourself from those who inhabit this dump.

You know what? I'm sick of making excuses for other people's idiocy. They should be made responsible for their actions. If they're allowed to keep going unpunished, of course they're going to continue playing up, eh? Takes just one strong individual to make an example of them, and they might just get the message to think twice before opening their mouths. But few have the brainpower to work this out. I've a good mind to be that man. About time folk round here took me seriously, and I don't mean in terms of being a threat. People are scared of being left behind. Okay, I'm not exactly setting the world on fire, but that's the thing. I'll do it in my own time, and not when anybody tells me to. What they fail to see is that being creative doesn't just happen overnight. Many have said that I should get a proper job. Most would give their right arm to have a career they really enjoyed.

I aspire to do better than others think I'm capable of. Coming up with something totally original is almost as good as sex. Like being God in a way. You can't bottle the feeling that comes with seeing your work in bright lights along the writers' promenade.

How about I give him the benefit of the doubt? Give him chance to explain once sober. Don't think so. This shouldn't have happened in the first place. It's not as if we're dealing with some eighteen-year-old ned. The culprit's a sixty-year-old man, who's expecting a baby by his thirty-something girlfriend any day now. Should know better. He has to realise that he's got responsibilities in the not-so-distant future – responsibilities that bring about certain sacrifices. For a start, Jack the Lad has got to be put to bed. Then, giving his newborn child the right outlook on life is next.

Respecting others, whether you agree with what they say or do, is a must. I don't live by anyone's rules – just my own. I'd like to think I have enough sense to let people live their life, even if it's not how I would go about things. Then again, I wouldn't feel much of a friend if I didn't voice my concerns to my nearest and dearest. If they take on board what I've advised but then decide not to use it, then so be it. Can't then accuse me of not caring.

Why can't people do that with me – express what they think of who I am? Wait a minute… I'm deflecting the purpose of why I'm actually having this conversation with myself in the first place. I'm trying to understand why people feel the need to continuously bug me. Maybe it's they who have the problem, not me. These tossers usually have more troubles than the people they bully. Why can't they all be like Jacko, and come out for nothing but a good crack. Too many look for a rumble, although not everyone's the same – just a select few. We know who they are – can spot them a mile away. Maybe they'll grow up. There's no point in saying anything, unless they want to change themselves. The change has to come from them. Can take a horse to water, but you can't make it drink. I've decided. Nothing can be as bad as the way I'm feeling now. Things will get better, though I don't want to keep having to get over things. It's not a life. It's more like being on death row. A ticking detonator with no idea of when's one sanctuary will arrive.

How about now – when I step out of the toilet? I've often tried to envisage what victims of 9/11 were thinking, knowing that the seconds before the plane crashed into one of the Twin Towers would ultimately be their last. Must be a bit of a buzz to go out in a blaze of glory. Can't believe it's all just doom and gloom. For me that kind of ending would be a fitting tribute to me as a person. I deserve a nice twist to my legacy. It's funny how up until you lift the lid of your coffin, and the minister asks you to get in, we never actually accept we have nothing to do with our own death. All think that we're going to live forever. No point in beating ourselves up about things in the past that we did or didn't do. Doesn't really matter a Scooby when we're on the verge of solving the biggest myth of all… where we go after passing over.

I'm an atheist, and have been ever since I could walk and talk unaided. People who need to believe in something, whether real or not, are severely lacking purpose in their lives. I've not attended church for about twelve years, but that's not me saying guidance beyond this realm ain't a possibility. I'd rather see it first hand before making judgement. This universe ain't all it's cracked up to be. Numerous aspects of life I detest. Things which one man like myself will never change single-handed. We're fighting a losing battle if any of us think that altering the mindset of the world as a whole is childsplay. We'll never see a time where everyone gets on. What a shame. Wouldn't wish this false existence of hope on my worst enemy, never mind your own flesh and blood. I'd love to be a fly on the wall to look back on every second of my life – resting in peace, knowing I'd have done nothing differently on examining the evidence.

Now we've got that sorted, it's time to put in place the finishing touches to my plan. Fasten your seatbelt, Lee, it's going to be a bumpy ride.

'Hey guys, how does this sound?'
    'What?'
    'I'm standing alone, I'm watching you all, and I'm seeing you sinkin'. I'm standing alone, you're weighing the gold, and I'm watching you sinking.'

Mind Games

For some, school is a rather stressful occupation. My guidance teacher couldn't stem the flow of verbal diarrhoea that my bullies were producing, so a chap called Guy Stokes from The Wilton Centre, Hawick received the too-hot-to-handle chalice that was much more poisonous than the England Manager's post. For an hour a week, normally a Wednesday – when I could skip one lesson of double Higher Religious Education – I'd pinpoint areas of my life that needed to be sorted out.

This was my first exposure to counselling and the mental health profession, and I was fairly surprised at how Guy genuinely wanted to help me to get back on the straight and narrow – if I was ever there in the first place. Though I only saw him for a year, in the room beside 'Computing One', I built up the kind of relationship with this man that is never likely to come about again. It never cost me a penny, but I and Andrew Lincoln (Egg in This Life) have more in common than he might think! There were daft wee things – like when it was Easter, Guy brought a Cadbury's Crème Egg to the session as a present for me. It was the thought that counted, and I was gutted when we had to part ways as I was leaving school. So many people I had known and trusted there just upped and left when they wanted, leaving me to pick up the pieces.

This was probably the first time I'd talked about my past in any great depth with anyone, stranger or otherwise. Getting all the fears, worries, and confusion off my chest was like having gold dust sprinkled over me and becoming a newborn person to boot.

Guy went to live in his wife's homeland of Germany not long after we said 'auf wiedersehen'. A few years later, I met him in Duns Market Square, when he got my age wrong by quite a margin. Guy, wherever you are now, you are forgiven!

He was one of those blokes who was not too concerned about what people thought of him, and he was the sort who I'd look upon as being a proper mate, if it were not for the counsellor/client relationship. Yes, that's right, there had to be no inappropriate contact outside the link formed. (Sorry, I am trying to make light of another situation that arose for me with a support organization which I will not name, and one of their volunteers, Susan.)

After finishing school, I lost a bit of my identity somewhat – going nowhere in particular, apart from a dole queue on Wednesday and Thursday mornings three times a month to collect my disability benefit. People have a tendency to look down their noses at others less fortunate, especially those on 'the social'. Guess what? I wasn't spared from jibes that were specially created to make you feel worthless. And so, although the 'couch potato' calling was put into jeopardy every weekend when I went to watch Paul play football for Duns Legion U-14s, going to my pit in the small hours and rising at lunch became routine. A 'Neighbours junkie' wasn't something I'd ever envisaged for myself, yet I fell into that laziness syndrome of just not being bothered.

This thrust Mum into a gun-slinging face-off between her and myself to see where I was going in life. She told me in no uncertain terms that if I didn't get a job and pay for my keep, then my bags would be packed and the apron strings cut. This was to try and get me to take responsibility for the time I'd been given here. Showing that I was making an effort was as much as I was willing to budge. The fish factory, where the majority of the people in the surrounding area were employed, seemed reluctant to entertain me, believing that the offer of manual work meant I would be a liability, because I didn't have full use of my arms and legs. I actually spoke to Stephanie Green, a girl I used to go to school with, on the phone at the reception desk, whose pep talk cheered me up no end. There was hardly any point in applying for a vacancy, then, eh? Considering most work there, it was sod's law that I should be turned away with such gusto.

In my heart I'd always wanted to be a writer, and I had no interest in chasing any other dream. Rowing with my mother led her to contact Fenton Lodge, to see if they could assist in why I was sinking my head in the sands, feeling sorry for myself. A Dr Brian Lescott and his temporary sidekick, Rachel Tennant, who was on work placement, came to the house, where they quickly ruled out the possibility that I was clinically depressed. And a few sessions of therapy with Rachel were supposed to get me back to my old self. I had to head back to the start and go over old ground, like when I saw Guy.

Just as I began to click with Rachel and feel as though I was getting somewhere, Rachel's time at the Lodge was up, and she went back to

Dundee. Although I had known that there was a strong probability she wouldn't be staying, I gave Rachel all I had in terms of the baggage I unloaded. Then Arlene McKinlay took over the reins, and I was at square one again. Nothing ever seemed to get sorted out as I kept reliving the past with each person.

Arlene was arguably the worst of the lot – a college course her solution to my woes. The only hitch was when I stepped off that bus at five thirty, the warts would still be waiting to crawl from within the surface of my flesh. I wanted some continuity, and not to be treated like a commodity on a conveyer belt. Arlene gave up on me. That broke the trend, although I hid my ecstasy at her bailing out. I really was quite pleased. I just didn't have the heart to say that I was fed up with the way things were.

Being too passive is how I've become the way I am today. I can't put across to people what I want or don't want, leaving me lost at sea. I've always thought I'm a misunderstood individual, although in some respects we all are – but me more than most. As I've grown up, being assertive has become easier. Just as long as your tone of voice fits the bill, then you realise people won't snap.

By now I was working my way through the whole local mental health service, and Peter Howarth from the social work department was the next name that was added to my CV. Many have a list of qualifications they've amassed, but I have a set of names the length and breadth of the Nile, and about as useful as a publican without drink for his thirsty customers. Peter went down the same path as Arlene, insisting that college was the answer to the ordeals I'd been through. To my relief, he too vanished as quickly as he had appeared, taking up a post in Hexham, Northumberland.

Jim McGoldrick travelled from Musselburgh to Duns everyday to work in and around the Borders as an occupational therapist. More hands-on than the rest, Jim's methods were essentially about what aspects of my life did to me, and what I wanted to change. He took me to public places such as the Pewter Plate Coffee Shop, to build up my self-confidence and interaction with new people. They say that the world is a small place, and on one of these occasions, while munching into a full English breakfast, Mum and a colleague from the bank, Julie, disrupted the exercise. Brash, is how I would describe their behaviour – just waltzing past as though I wasn't even there. It was the first time Jim had seen Mum – never mind been formally introduced! There were a few times when I spoke too loudly. Jim advised me to keep it low, as what I was telling him wasn't for just anybody's ears.

Closely following on from Guy, Jim got the most out of me, for which he has my unwavering thanks. He not only showed me that I could peel a potato or open a bottle on my own – with a device built specially for these things – but also he helped me to create an image of the sort of life I certainly longed for. I remember how he had a very distinctive voice, which whenever I remember it always makes me giggle.

The recurring pattern of support network changing the guard again came when Jim reluctantly left me to my own devices to take up a position nearer to home. He put me in the capable hands of a voluntary organisation for young people with mental health difficulties. To start with things were okay, but it was… well, you can guess the drill. Yep, I had to go through all that garbage again! Do these people never keep notes, I thought! Kathy Livermore, like Peter and Jim, saw me at the flat mostly. A drop-in on Wednesday nights, where fellow clients and I could meet, was also up for grabs. A similar idea in Kelso on Friday afternoons was made available shortly afterwards. I used to get an old man from Duns to take me there because public transport is pitiful. Eventually, the timetable fitted my requirements, and I was able to make my own way there on the bus.

I also saw a French lady called Josette from In Touch in Galashiels. These appointments were carried out in the local contact centre. I warmed to Kathy in the same way as I had to Guy, Rachel and Jim. It's true what they say… you can please some of the people some of the time, but not all of the people all of the time. I was delighted that I'd found yet another person to confide in, although as time went on, the more I got the feeling that Kathy was trying to turn me against my mother.

As a treat, we were taken to a holiday house in Dunbar, a stone's throw away from the High Street. For three nights and two days, Bob Murdoch from Hawick, Jill Notman from Kelso and Lizzie Mills from Berwick were my younger companions. I felt out of place, if nothing else, but was prepared to give it a go, knowing that they, like me, had come from topsy-turvy backgrounds. Understandably, I can't go into the questions of 'who/why/where/what' regarding the loveless pasts they'd had, but whatever I'd been through was surely nothing compared with their problems.

With hindsight, maybe I never gave them a proper chance, opting to distance myself from kids who I perceived to be delinquents. In particular, Bob was quite a rogue – trying to impress Jill and Lizzie with his silly talk. He had no idea that Lizzie batted for the other side, or that Jill was seeing someone. If he did know, he was probably just investing in some harmless flirting to make time fly by. I sort of had an inclination, but like most of the straight population, I didn't like to ask or assume. It's funny how we let these issues prey on our minds, until someone slips up.

The first night focussed on getting to know one another through party games. There were no set plans for our mini-break, and we even had to make some of our meals – all part of the living-on-your-own movement. Sharing a room with Bob was an experience I'm not going to forget lightly.

I must say that my favourite bit of the three days was when we headed to North Berwick for the afternoon. Hopping on a boat to do the Bass Rock tour – bottle-nosed dolphins swimming alongside us on our trip was absolutely breathtaking. Bob, an amateur cameraman for the day, caught all this for posterity. On our last evening, we were asked to write a word, phrase or sentence to sum up the person to our right. When finished, you'd fold the piece of paper and pass it to the left, so they could do the same. It went round the circle until you had the original piece of paper. To top off the whole assignment, the scary part was reading out loud what the others had written about you. It was easy to see who had written what. After all, Bob's details were left underneath his description.

This was my first venture out of Duns for more than five years since I'd gone to Malta, and I thought it would be the last time I saw any of my companions. Lauren had stopped coming to the Kelso drop-in at the Dry Bar and was too quiet for my liking, while Bob lived three quarters of an hour away, and wasn't really my cup of tea, although he was all right for seeing in small doses. Lizzie sent me a letter a while after we went our separate ways, although I never replied. I don't know why. Everyone I met – including the brother and sister, Mitchell and Liza Johnson, from Eyemouth – I just didn't connect with. I tried my best, but found them all too below my level. Sounds harsh, eh? They weren't bad people. It's just that I couldn't imagine being mates with them. Maybe that's my loss at the end of the day. Four years have come and gone without contact from any of them whatsoever. Can't say that I'm too heartbroken, though I hope they're doing okay and have turned their lives around. There was one fella I thought I could have been good pals with, but Micah had a phobia of talking on the phone, so nothing was ever arranged. Even when we gabbed at Eyemouth, as it came to the end of the night he could never agree to doing something outside the drop-in, claiming he liked to do stuff when he felt like it, rather than be disappointed at something pre-planned.

In October 2001, I had a long hard look at my situation with support organisations and figured that I didn't want to be mucked about too much longer. Instead of being someone they wanted to help, I slipped into obscurity, like the doggy in the window waiting for someone to give it a squirt of tender loving care. A wind-up tin soldier ordered to march to the top of the hill was not my idea of how life should be lived. Kathy's little helpers, Joss Walters and Steven McCall, were equally as smothering, though Steven relented somewhat, knowing that he couldn't sway me to their way of thinking. They didn't predict I'd see through the rose-tint in their glasses. That's what they hated me for – having a mind of my own. I wasn't prepared to accept their mumbo jumbo. I'd air my opinion, whether or not they wanted to hear it.

I met Joss for a coffee in the Pewter Plate in November of the same year – my last lecture, before easing the nails on the cross. I'd now be released from the excruciating battle of wits. Joss' attempt to dilapidate me left him spitting out bullets, simply because I wasn't giving in to his blackmail. As I got up to leave, he was still trying to put me under his thumb. The tenacity of the man – to think that their work with me was far from finished is irritating to say the least, and candidly speaking, the only domain in which I've ever felt I've been able to be myself is when supporting Aberdeen Football Club.

****

My initiation for the Red and White Barmy Army came on Saturday 13th April 1991, when we played against Heart of Midlothian at Tynecastle,

Edinburgh. Going to the match was an early present for my 11th birthday, which falls on the 21st of that month. In Religious Education a couple of years later, we were asked to write an essay describing the day in our life we'd most enjoyed. The game, and everything that went with it, was what I wrote about. In her appraisal, Mrs Robinson said that it was well written, and I still have the jotter that the assignment is in. It was bad enough that Rob slept in, although what I didn't expect was for us to get stuck in a traffic jam. I knew what time kick-off was, but not how far we were from the stadium. I'd followed the fortunes of the Dandy Dons for the previous two years, and I had always dreamt how I wanted my first match to go – without any hitches!

We were sitting in our seats well before the 3 p.m. start, yet the diehard casuals, heard from the Main Stand behind the goal, kept me entertained until the teams stripped for action. The warm-up didn't really do anything for me. This is the sort of thing you don't get to see when watching a game on the TV. Capturing the atmosphere is what does it for me. I've never understood why I feel more relaxed between thousands of fans than I do talking to people I know to chatter to and see most days of the week. I have an idea though. Is it because I'm never judged? We were all there for the same reason – to cheer on our team. Each has a different story to tell of how it was down to our chanting the many nutty songs on terraces across the country in all kinds of weather as to whether there was a win, lose or draw.

My fellow 'sheepshaggers' are people who have always sent shivers down the spine. Their continuous optimism of getting back to the dawn of Alex Ferguson is something that never dies. Yet there is a proudness in the club and its heritage that players of the past have failed to grasp. We don't turn up in our thousands to see overpaid androids going through malfunction each week. We want to share the good old days with them, just as much as they want to relive them for us. We're supposed to be in it together, and whatever anguish they suffer through disappointment, we probably feel it just as hard, because no one player is, or should be, bigger than the fans. Nobody says that we demand success after our untouchable history, but what we do deserve is a team on the pitch who gives their all. If we were then to win nothing, at least we can say we're lucky to have a side so committed to the people who matter most. Either that, or the better team won on the day. I don't think we've ever asked for a lot, just an honest set of lads prepared to wear the jersey with pride. Fans can be fickle at the best of times, and when we went 1-0 down to a Stewart McKimmie O.G., the tone of my then new groupie mates changed ever so slightly.

However, by full time, with goals from McKimmie (yes, in the right net!), Dutch poacher Hans Gillhaus, and two via Robert Connor, my love affair with the Dandies had well and truly begun. Over the next two and a half years, my weekends were primarily spent checking the fortunes of the only team in the Granite City. Depending on how well they fared, it determined what mood I'd be in for the rest of the week, or until they next played. I could be a living hell to be with, or the best company anyone could wish for. Mum never needed to attend church, with all the praying she did in any case – trying to muster an Aberdeen win, come quarter to five on a Saturday afternoon. For me, it was the end of the world if we lost, especially if we'd scored no goals. Now, as I'm hopefully a little bit wiser with age, I can understand why I felt this way. When you have nothing else in life to occupy your brain, it's no wonder that the law of averages results in a swing of the state of mind. Madness, and all because the team you follow hasn't won! As priorities have changed throughout time, the issue of whether Aberdeen win or not has become less important, although not totally redundant. I go to games today just to enjoy the moment, and I accept the day's events for what they're worth.

Some of the greatest experiences of my life have come through watching football's most northern kings. This is sad to say, but true. I won't go down that road too much here, as I could write a book dedicated to talking about my spiritual journey with the men whose homes lie in the heady lights (or should that be heady heights?) of Scotland's third largest city.

I learned the biggest, most valuable, lesson I'm ever likely to learn at a Hibernian vs Aberdeen game outside Easter Road in the winter of 1999. It was the first game I'd gone to on my own, and the first time I'd been on a bus and train by myself. Not bad for a nineteen-year-old, eh? Wasn't looking forward to it one bit, although the adrenaline and excitement of seeing my heroes was enough to see me through the anxiety of being alone, doing the thing I most loved. I'd gathered that this wasn't the way it was supposed to be at a football match, but knew that whatever happened on the day itself, getting to know the person I was inside was a bigger buzz than any three points collected. A minor drawback was not being able to sport my colours. Such a course of action was just too dangerous. Not wearing the colours was the price I had to pay for wanting to root for the boys in red. The highlight of the whole trek was getting a wave from Eoin Jess, Paul Bernard, Andy Dow and Robbie Winters as the team coach drove past me on Leith Walk. We lost the game 2-0 – Pat McGinlay and ex-Aberdeen Finnish striker Mixu Paatelainen grabbing the limelight.

Foolishly, I put on my Dennis the Menace Aberdeen hat (as some have called it), until I got home. What with getting beat, I thought that no one would bother me. How careless can one man be? Just before crossing Princes Street to head into Edinburgh Waverley, two Hibee's taunted me with V sign gestures as they passed, to show what I'd just seen with my very own eyes – my team losing 2-0! I might have understood their behaviour if Aberdeen had won 2-0, yet I guess it comes with the territory. I choose not to gloat in public when we've secured a super-duper three points. The barracking didn't stop there, and went a bit too far, claiming, as I descended the steps leading into the station, that they hoped my train would crash on the way home. Drink almost certainly played a part in their actions, but was no excuse for their stupidity.

I had a couple of hours to spare before my train to Berwick-upon-Tweed, so went for a bite to eat in the Burger King opposite the ticket office. I placed my order – a Whopper, fries and large Coke – and picked up the tray to scan the room for a seat. It's strange how when you get something into your head and believe it enough it usually comes true. Well, I knew that my left hand, no matter how good a grip I got on the tray, wasn't strong enough to carry it to a table. I smile when remembering how everything spilled onto the floor. Three fellow Aberdeen fans erased any embarrassment I felt by winking and telling me that if it wasn't bad enough that I'd spent twenty pounds watching an abysmal Aberdeen team it'd been topped by throwing my tea on the ground. My food was replaced by staff behind the counter, but with all my senses on red alert, I lifted the tray again and finally won a spot on one of those calamity video-clip programmes hosted by a Z-list celebrity whose flagging career needs a boost of some sort. Yep, I dropped it a second time. Everyone who witnessed both accidents saw the funny side of my fifteen minutes of fame. Eventually a member of the BK franchise took my meal to a table of my choice.

Joking aside, I can see why it happened to me not just once, but twice. Answer? I was too scared to admit that I needed help. I'd been hell-bent on showing everyone that I could cope on my own, but now was the time to concede defeat and acknowledge the truth that I may require assistance with certain tasks in life. It also taught me not to be ashamed of myself with the disability I have. I had no say in the matter of its existence, and people should and probably do know that this is something that comes as part of the Lee package and isn't going away any time soon. Whether they're uncomfortable with it I don't know, but if they are they don't show it. Ed, one of my dearest friends of over eleven years, once said to me: 'I sometimes have to remind myself that you're disabled.' Cracks me up every time I recite that quietly. What a thing to say. Must be a compliment of some kind for the way in which I carry my body.

Striking while the iron was hot, I hopped on the train home, using what I now knew. Spoke to the station guard, and explained that I may not be able to open the door to depart at Berwick-upon-Tweed. Almost eight years on, I remember Ronnie Coats getting one of his colleagues to escort me to the first class carriage. It was only a fifty-minute ride, but they wanted to make sure I got off at my stop, so put me in first class – a place where they'd be able to do their job.

Between 1993 and 1996, Rob, Paul and I became season ticket holders at Pittodrie. On match days, this exercise used to take near to twelve hours to watch just a ninety-minute game! On an odd occasion, we'd travel to Hermiston during the Friday night in the car to sleep at our Uncle Rob's and Jack's house. It meant that we could spend an extra hour in bed and be an hour closer to our second home. The train would leave Edinburgh Waverley at 10.22, and arrive in Aberdeen at 13.50. Wouldn't leave Aberdeen till 18.15, and got back to Edinburgh for 20.45. We then had an hour's drive to Duns, which if confronted by bad weather or any other obstacles, saw us come to a halt at near ten. And all for a bloody football match! People wouldn't understand our dedication to a team whose glory years were sadly overshadowing future exploits. But it got me out of Duns for most of the weekend – which was beneficial to my development as a person. And it made sure that I was equipped to deal with the real world.

Duns never has provided, and never will provide, a life for me – just an existence. It seems to me that the people of this town know nothing.

They only see what they watch on TV, read in the papers, or listen to on the radio. That's why I now treat most of what they say with a pinch of salt. Their opinions aren't worth a dime. Should keep them to themselves and save their breath. I don't want to hear them anymore. I have a tendency to come out fighting when the chips are down – especially making people's eyes pop from the sockets with some surprising results.

I'd always told Mum that I'd twinkle-toe the Pittodrie turf one day. I just didn't know how or when! It's something I definitely remember doing, though details are a little sketchy, and possibly a bit inaccurate! Before the game had kicked off, players at the Merkland Family Stand were signing autographs for kids. Having taken half an hour to realise this, I leapt from my seat to jump at the chance of getting Joe Miller's scribble – as most players actually do scribble, that is. Might be the Sultan of Brunei's signature for all we know! There were only a couple of lads and lassies to go before it was my turn, and Mr Miller decided it was time to get on with his lonesome warm-up schedule. The winger, who was never a model of consistency, and rarely after the running and stretching drills, messed about with the rest of the squad. Then some lad, who I'd never met before, asked me to open the fire exit gate as we were going to see our number seven. I was nothing short of heavenly in my younger years, and wasn't getting a criminal record for the sake of some overrated footballer. Okay, I might have got a caution for a first offence, but I wasn't taking any chances! Persistent as hell, this scumbag threatened to go it alone. Well, I thought, if I was ever going to tread the hallowed turf in a replica strip, now was the time.

'Fuck appearances!' I proclaimed to whoever was listening as this nutter and me navigated the advertising boards like Olympic 110 metre hurdles competitors. To run on a pitch that has seen many glorious nights was equivalent of being in your own bubble. Nothing was stopping me now that I'd started. Everything seemed to be in slow motion – like a box office blockbuster about to untangle. The infamous Sylvester Stallone scene where Rocky Balboa demolishes his cocky adversary Apollo Creed to take the Heavyweight title is a classic example of what I mean. You know what the outcome is, but you just don't know how you're going to get there! Managing to catch Joe's attention, he went into that 'stern policeman' mode of reading the riot act by telling us what would happen if the stewards caught us breaking stadium safety rules! We turned our backs so that the programmes had something smooth to lean on as two more grateful worshippers got their hands on a piece of priceless memorabilia. Whilst having mine signed, I clocked Rob and Paul in the crowd and gave them a wave. I still don't know what was running through their heads as I played out my own version of what a ball boy's responsibilities were. Sprinting isn't one of my favourite pastimes, so let's say I lapped up every moment while I returned from dreamland to reality and back to my seat. I can accomplish anything in life if applying myself like I did that afternoon. Never thought about doing it, and the potential punishment if spotted. I had just got on with it. The most natural and exhilarating thing I've ever done! To think that at the tender age of fourteen or fifteen I had that fearless side to my personality in the locker. For people on the outside, it should almost be like watching a different person. And it was a big eye-opener to me to see that I was made of the stuff I thought I was made of. It boosted my self-confidence to the hilt, and that event is probably the pinnacle of my life so far.

A close second must be the 6-5 thriller at Fir Park, Motherwell, on Wednesday 20th October 1999. After the break-up of Rob and Mum's marriage, I went to no games over a period of two years. Having been to ninety-four in six years, I guess it had become a way of life, and I was bound to miss it. I certainly did – feeling as though I'd lost a large chunk of my identity. The inability to drive, and having no friends that supported the team, a lack of any financial resources and a dire local transport service ultimately condemns you to the part-time fan directory.

Something I take great pride in is the fact I'm not just an armchair follower. I love the unpredictability of Aberdeen. A bit like me, you never know which Aberdeen will turn up. Don't try and be someone, just be yourself – then there's no way you can create disappointment. That's what I've stopped doing – trying to be someone I'm not for the sake of others, although I've never done anything just to fit in, whatever fitting in means.

One Wednesday morning, I had the urge just to get out of Duns for the night. So I phoned Rob, who lived six miles away in Chirnside and was unemployed at the time. He thought an evening match supporting my beloved reds sounded like a great idea, especially as we both needed a pick-me-up. My mum's third husband, Gordon, drove to where Rob was collecting me, and then the fun began. When we got to Lanarkshire,

I had this feeling that there was something special brewing. It was the stop/start rain that gave it away! Must have been mad to chuck nearly seventy pounds down the drain on some no-hopers in the sphere of their chosen profession. You see, Aberdeen hadn't won under new Danish boss Ebbe Skovdahl, who like me was certainly a character, while the Steelmen were having a difficult time of it too, with one win in nine. We had to wait just three minutes before Andy Dow drew first blood with an aided deflection from Tony Thomas. I'd got something for my eighteen pound admission, but then again I wasn't ready for what was about to take place. Eight minutes gone, and Robbie Winters doubled our lead as every one of the 250+ people who were scattered about the lower half of the away end rubbed their eyes to gaze at the electronic scoreboard to get their heads round what was actually happening. I'd have settled for slamming the door shut and preserving the 2-0 lead for a good three points on the road. Even if both goals were scored at the opposite end from where we were sitting. John Spencer spoiled that thought when twisting and turning Norwegian stopper Thomas Solberg on the edge of the box to reduce Well's arrears to just one with only twenty minutes on the clock. Winters restored the two-goal advantage eight minutes later, latching on to an Andreas Mayer trickler that rebounded off a post, Robbie reacting quickest to silence three quarters of the ground. I saw Eoin Jess score one of his last goals for the club on forty- one minutes – to increase the scope of victory. Bulgarian firecracker, Ilian Kiriakov, squared it to Jess twenty yards from goal. He took one touch and thumped it past Andy Goram, and we were now certainly getting value for money! Don Goodman, looking suspiciously like a '70s reggae idol, continued the freakish live entertainment, by poking in from close range a few minutes before the interval. At half time, everyone in the Aberdeen end was so buzzing that it was like no other fifteen minutes in my life. I was just so happy that we were watching our team winning at a canter – except that by the final whistle, to people hearing of the score, thoughts that a bunch of school kids had taken to the field might not have been too far away. Shortly after the break, Winters angered the claret and amber by bagging his hat-trick amid calls that he was offside, although Andy Dow never touched the ball as Robbie timed his run to perfection. Spencer fooled Solberg again when notching his brace to cement the game into SPL chronicle. Paul Bernard put the finishing touches to a fantastic team move on sixty-eight minutes – a goal that sparked bedlam in the finest fashion.

We were like giddy teenage girls who'd finally got the chance to meet our favourite boy band. Spencer completed his treble with a cute header beyond an unprotected Jim Leighton. Shaun Teale then stroked a penalty into the bottom corner, and this unbelievable match had written it's last chapter. I'll remember that night for the rest of my life. It'll be hard to beat – put it that way. When Jess made it 4-1, a guy sitting next to us made me laugh. When everyone else had sat down in his or her seat, this man was standing up, rubbing his behind. I heard his mate say: 'Graeme why aren't you sitting down?' And the reply was 'My arse is sore! In all the time I've watched Aberdeen, I've never seen them score more than one goal in a game, and here we are a few minutes before half time and we've got four!'

Leaving the ground after celebrating with the players is also something I will never forget – a moment in time that's embedded in my memory forever. Singing 'The Northern Lights Of Old Aberdeen' until we parted for our cars and buses was a perfect cessation to a wonderful night. I could talk about the time I urinated down my trouser leg in a phonebox outside Halfords (the reason being that I was desperate to go, while Rob was on the blower to Mum telling her we'd reached our destination safely). The conversation seemed to go on forever, which subsequently resulted in a puddle seeping onto the road where a busy roundabout stood. Or I could tell again about when a Chief Inspector in the Cow Shed with no shelter to save me getting wet rearranged my yellow binbag from having my arms through the leg holes and legs through the arm holes to the right way round!

The only other game remotely worth discussing is the one that Paul and I went to on our own. Yes, it was at my second-favourite ground behind Fir Park – Easter Road again. For me, it was the beginning of us starting to live life, rather than letting our adversities overcome us. I'd allowed them to shackle my every move, but this game with little brother is what I thought we should have been doing since the minute we got parole. That's right – life with the man who had created us was very hard.

On the Friday, after finalising my travel arrangements for the day, I threw a hissy fit at Mum for trying to get Paul to come along. I thought he would spoil it, although looking back he probably almost certainly made the day what it was. It felt terrific getting to know my sibling for who he'd become since the great escape when compared with how I had known him when we were just two innocent kids who had been unaware of exactly what we were going through. He was now sixteen and I was twenty, and I felt that as long as we had each other I could take on the world without fear. Because I knew where I was going, I was kind of swollen with pride – protecting my hero. Yet he was well capable of looking after himself at that age. We managed to bag seats two rows from the top – the hardcore fans were just a few feet away, bawling loudly. Played Hibs off the park that afternoon, but didn't get the two goals till late on. In one of the best performances from an Aberdeen team I've seen, master of the offside trap, the Norwegian Arild Stavrum, netted the first, and German maestro Andreas Mayer the second, in injury time. The clincher incited the most hair-raising celebrations I've ever had the good fortune to be part of. Everything in the stand shook, and for a split second I thought that the construction or I would fall in a heap on the floor. The noise spawned gave me my very own account of what it's like to be legless. I couldn't sit down, as my left leg wobbled like jelly, while the right did its best impersonation of being under anaesthetic. Not a great combination, let me tell you! People always talk of the fanatical support Manchester United, Arsenal, Liverpool, Newcastle United, Celtic and Rangers get. That day, although there were relatively few of us, it confirmed for me that if we can return to the halcyon days, we could compete with the so-called big guns of world football, our fan base being second to none. That's why I challenge anyone to go to an Aberdeen away match and not enjoy themselves, regardless of our result.

You've never lived until experiencing first hand the kind of effect it has on someone as multifaceted as I am. The game has given me what most people never find in life – two of the best friends anyone could ever ask for. I can't thank Ed Davidson and Joe McKelvey enough for sticking by me through the highs and the lows of the past twelve years. Hope I've been just as good for you lads! You'd have to meet these two to see why I see them more as brothers than anything else. And although they are now doing their own thing in the city of Edinburgh, I'm secure in the knowledge that they'll always have time for me, whatever our circumstances. As long as they're around for the important bits, then I'm happy for them to explore life as they see fit.

****

I first met John, a lanky git, whilst playing football with Paul, Rob and a few others down in the public park. You know the score when there's more than one group of kids dreaming of being the next David Beckham, Michael Owen or Wayne Rooney. Once the egos are laid to one side, a massive match is on the go, and usually the team with the more skilful players wins by about fifteen goals. The opposition has given up before starting, claiming how unfair it is to have so many good players on the same side. Wouldn't like to count the amount of hours we wasted arguing our corner to repick teams! We planned on playing for five to six hours every Friday night, all Saturday and Sunday afternoons, and any school holidays – yet only ran our heads off like headless chickens for about two! How did we ever come back so dirty? The running joke in those days was what time did Joe and his brother, Stuart, have to be in, each time we got together. When it was a good night they could stay out till 7.45 p.m. And that was extended to quarter past eight during holidays. If it happened to be a bad night it was 7.15 p.m. on the dot, or else there'd be trouble! For a boy of Joe's teenage years this seemed a major embarrassment, but to be honest it didn't really bother the rest of us because in time we've found JAM (Joe Arsehole McKelvey) to be a top bloke!

I already knew wavy-haired ex-child model Ed who went to school with Paul. After the breakdown of his parent's marriage, he was to stay at my house with his mother Judy and younger sisters, Ruth and Alice, for a few months until they were allocated a home of their own. Rob and Mum split in May 1997, and the house at weekends was never her own again! Without parental guidance we could do whatever we wanted as long as we kept the decibel levels down. The Happy Mondays have a song called 24-Hour Party People. Well, stick another forty-eight on top of that, as we treated the place like someone holding a weekend bender. There was no alcohol, but we had so many things to occupy us that it didn't really matter. Whether it was watching videos, playing games on the P.C. and Playstation, eating, and drinking fizzy juice until we got fat, or the CD player on the go, all three floors were used. That's what I loved about it – the fact that the relationships between each of us blossomed because we weren't in one another's faces all of the time.

Familiarity might have bred contempt if we'd not allowed the troupe to do their own thing when they wanted. This crazy epoch lasted for nearly three years – until I moved into my own flat at Glebe Court, and the others spread their wings and made plans to flit the nest too.

Fenwick (Marcus Cuthbert), an acquaintance from Chirnside, rarely attended these sessions, as he'd joined the RAF fixing Chinook helicopters at wherever they posted him. Seth Robertson took off to Berwick-upon-Tweed with his mum, Denise, Uncle David and stepfather Ian, but hadn't been part of the gang long – a year if that, although he did keep in touch with my then best friend Izzy McIntosh for a while. Izzy lost my trust and complete respect in March 1999, but the story of that can wait, as it'll spoil what I have to say about my two best mates.

On one of these all-nighters we'd decided to play football the following day once everyone was *compos mentis*, though that morning I just knew I'd be as much use as a chocolate fireguard, so opted to hover in my bed. I don't know whether I'd ever told Joe that I'd slept in the nude since I was thirteen or fourteen. If I had, he must have forgotten. When he made the decision it was time for me to get up, Joe came into my room and whipped the duvet onto the floor to reveal me in all my glory – the birthday suit! This was a sight that could have traumatised Joe for some time, and it's something we still talk about with a degree of flippancy. Let's pray that he's the only man to see my genitals!

Joe and I will share a lot over the next couple of decades, though nothing as daft as the night it was just the two of us kipping in Paul and Craig's beds, playing Truth or Dare. My two brothers were in Penicuik for the weekend seeing Rob (Craig's dad) while Izzy and Ed were also visiting their fathers in Glasgow and Abbey St Bathans respectively. Hadn't met Seth at this point, but he too hasn't had his biological father full-time since he was two. Joe's dad died when he was fifteen – on Valentine's Day, 1997. Joe let me ask the first question as I was never dicey enough back then to take on or give a dare. He described the question as the best one anyone had ever asked him. Eventually, and after a lot of consideration, Joe gave me an answer I expected from the man who I believe can and will have all the things he wants in life. When we slipped into the land of Nod, I didn't anticipate forgetting Joe's answer or my question! It can't have been that great a question, eh? Seven years on, every time we meet to catch up, the first question on our lips is if either of us has remembered that question yet? And the answer is always no!

Sticks and Stones

The best comes to those who wait, but never did I think I'd see the day when I stood up to one of my bullies. In the summer of 2002, I met some 'workies' from Uddingston, Glasgow, who became very protective of me after catching a glimpse of how I was treated by some of the locals. If I hadn't talked my new friends out of it, a few would have been decked – with questions asked later. They stayed in the White Swan for nearly three months, and were even introduced to Mum and Gordon when laying the cables under the pavement for the town's CCTV system outside their home in Langtongate. For befriending them, they bought innumerable cans of ginger (Coke) for me, and bottles of Carlsberg for Karen the barmaid – who also did their dry-cleaning. Apparently we were the only two to give them a chance, and Duns didn't know what had hit it when they finished for the day or weekend – as they knew very well how to enjoy themselves.

I got to know the central four pretty well, and was even invited up to their quarters once or twice. Oasis was never off George's CD player – which sometimes drove the others bananas! They were all slightly crazy in one way or another, but they accepted me into their camp without asking for anything or my having to prove a thing. Wee Rab, who gave me his phone number and address before leaving, was like my mother and used to give me a row for not shaving. If he thought I looked like a scruff, then God only knows what everyone else was thinking. He was clean-shaven himself, and very light on top – which might have had a lot to do with it! I didn't dare get on the wrong side of Rab, so did as I was told and scrubbed up like a trustworthy little boy. I knew that nothing bad would happen, and I just wanted to continue where I had started off with them – on good terms. James was the gaffer, and he thought that Mum was a bit of a hottie. I felt safe when he was around because although smaller than tough George, he was the kind of person you wouldn't want to meet in a dark alley. He could have a laugh and a carry on like the rest of them, but when it came to work being completed on time, the others didn't play up, as they knew that it was his neck that was on the line.

I was in the room on one occasion when some shouting was in full flow. It wasn't pretty, though possibly necessary. Dean, the youngest, took it all in his stride, and tried to do as little as possible, but mucked in when things were threatening to go against them – like not meeting certain deadlines! The crew thought he didn't want to spoil his boyish good looks – the kind that caught the eye of a lot of the local lassies, though he had sense to leave them alone. He somehow kept them at arm's length yet still messed with their heads.

I think that George showed me how to have fun before anyone else had. I was with him when he was sent on a pick-up job to get materials from Pearsons'. Once he got the stuff into the back of the truck, he asked me to show him the castle where inside scenes of 'Mrs Brown' had been filmed – the one with Billy Connolly and Dame Judi Dench. He wasn't interested in things like science fiction because it was about made-up things. He loved the history of the places he'd visited, so that he could learn about what it had been like before he arrived. I took him to the estate at the top of Castle Street, where you can go only so far before trespassing on private property, and there is a sign that reads, 'No unauthorised parties beyond this point.' There's not much of a view of the castle from the long driveway, so I suggested that we tried to get a better look from circling the lake. George had a mind of his own, and nothing was going to stop him from seeing it up close. Breaking the rules and the speed limit, we bolted along to the front of the castle within seconds. By the way it jumped along, the car reminded me of the one in the Dukes of Hazzard. He admired the castle for a couple of minutes, and then asked where the road veering off from the courtyard digs led. I said I didn't know, and he replied, 'Let's find out then!'

George was like the new Colin McCrae in the way that he took the bends and bumps. For the fifteen-minute ride, the makeshift rally car nearly hit a few trees and boulders along the way! Then we came to a clearing with no road to follow. George was disappointed, and our 'trial' was over for the Jim Clark Memorial – that took place in and around the closed roads of Berwickshire in the first week of July.

We went back the way we had come, and cruised out of the other entrance – next to the High School – without being captured by those who were obviously not watching from their thrones that day. To have done something forbidden and got away with it was something I'd never felt before, and I wasn't keen to try again. There are only so many times that you can get away with it, and it does get boring trying to be a fool to please a crowd. It's not me, and from my experience, the situation of being an idiot only gets you so far in life. That's not to say that I didn't appreciate George's unexpected silly turn. I did, and in addition I recognised that George seemed to need to do this sort of thing to keep him alive. Duns certainly didn't agree with 'Mr Celtic'.

All the workies looked after me – for which I'm lost for words. Just having their pictures on the Walls of Fame is enough to remember them by. The Walls of Fame are in my living room – where photos of all those who mean something to me, or who affected my life in some way, are on display. Everyone from family and friends to the celebrities I've met have their own place on one of the three walls.

Before they left, George gave me his Celtic baseball cap and told me to wear it with pride, and at all times – because he'd take it off me if he heard I wasn't! He didn't want it in a drawer or hung on a peg doing nothing – which it is now. However, I did bear it religiously for over six months – until the stick from people about it got so revolting. They couldn't understand why I, as an Aberdeen fan, could show such a public exhibition of disloyalty to the Dons. I knew the reasons behind the gift, so I wasn't that bothered about what they said. Why should I be? I'd rather have mates like George and Co., who lived life the way they wanted, than people who bitch about others when they're gone. Rab said if anyone in Duns was continually giving me shit, I was to phone the number he'd written down and most of Uddingston would come and sort it out in their vanloads. I thanked him for the kind offer, but warned him not to expect a call, as I'd deal with those that annoyed me like I always had – by letting the Lord see to the things they did, since any hate in my heart would consume me.

I quoted a certain Mr Will Smith – a man who for me has always had his head screwed on the right way. It doesn't surprise me that there's an element of coolness about him. His words are in one of my favourite Will tracks – 'Just The Two Of Us' – which, from the video, is clearly about him and his relationship with his son. It reminds me a lot about my father, and what I've never had with him or any other man – the really close union that all of us are entitled to with our parents. Rab said that I knew where they were if I ever needed them – which is a nice thing to fall back on. But I'd never solved my problems that way, and wasn't going to start then.

However, I used this offer to my psychological advantage a couple of years later. A particular individual who had done nothing but get on my nerves for almost twelve years just needed to be told. As I heard him comment on my teeth, and what you could do with the tombstones at the front, things had to be settled there and then, or they never would be. I walked over and asked him how old he was, as I thought that for a guy of twenty-four he wasn't really acting his age. I asked him how much longer he had to let his disease control the way he spoke to me. His response was to take me outside to finish things once and for all. This was in the same way as his brother had – because I wouldn't tell him if I was still a virgin or not. (Never knew my sex life was his or anyone else's business.) The foolish thing was that both these skirmishes couldn't be blamed on the drink, because they were stone-cold sober at the time, and each knew fine well what they were saying.

Going back to the first incident, this lad had got up to go for a fist fight, while I just sat and smiled at his attempt to be big in the company. I had never once wasted my breath, time or effort on this man before, so why would I now? He wasn't worth it. I told him all this, and that that is why I never stuck up for myself at school. I knew people who would do a job for me, so I didn't have to get my hands filthy. I couldn't believe that I was saying this, as I was sounding just as bad as he was, if not worse. It was just that something had to be said, and I thought that messing with his mind was the best option – except that now I'd raised the stakes a little, by edging a bit further into his psyche.

Maybe I had taken it too far, but I was sick and tired of having to put up with the nonsense people gave me. Maybe I should have set a trend the first time someone had a go – by either walking away while they spouted their garbage, thus making them look like the ass, or just verbally standing up for myself. I'd done neither in the past. The thing was that I had no intention of wasting money on a hitman, as his friends might say, but then he didn't know that. You see, this is the key, because he'd be keeping an eye out for anybody and anything that looked a tad suspicious that could lead to him being harmed. Harm was not what I intended, but I did want him to take me seriously.

As he left to go to another pub, he tried to laugh off my threat by giving me the address of his flat in Edinburgh where he was studying to be a P.E. teacher. I informed him that it didn't matter if he was leaving there soon, because address or no address they'd find him. And who said I was going to order them to go through with the operation in the next three weeks he said he'd be there? It'd come when he least expected it. Felt really great after confronting him with what could happen if he stepped out of line again. However, I'd be number one suspect if something were to happen between then and the next time I met him – because of my stunt in front of his mates, whom I knew too. In that case, I'd have to live by the sword and die by the sword. This brought about some paranoia on my part, and my plan seemed destined to backfire. After all, what if the tyres on his car were a little flat and caused a crash, in which he later lost his life? I would never have lived with the guilt.

I knew that there were a select few in Duns that needed bringing down a notch or two, and he was one of them. If some of the people had said what they had to some of my fellow Mancs, they'd have been kneecapped the proper way. Yes, I'm a bit eccentric, but I have a sensible side to me, which many from my neck of the woods don't. Cross them and their crazy minds, and you'd better start praying. I don't like anyone taking liberties and not thinking twice about getting rid of you. Okay, these people exist in lots of towns and cities around the country, but they probably wouldn't encounter people from Duns every day. As it panned out, I saw his pals again a week later in the same pub, and they gave me the good news. He was up working at the Rugby Club, but had been watching his back all week to make sure that my people weren't keeping close tabs on him before pouncing. I shook their hands, and thanked them for waving the white flag on his behalf. This was one battle where the war had well and truly been won by the noble ones. Now that I have the psychological hold back, he'll never get the better of me again. I don't want to be friends with him. I can do without friends like that, thank you very much. I've regained the control, and I find it quite amusing when he talks to me now as though he's been a great buddy over the years. The things he speaks about are of no concern to me, as he doesn't know to whom he's talking, though he now knows what I'm capable of – much more than he ever imagined.

****

It was while at school that I first tried to take my own life. The loneliness inside at not being understood by those around me was like a volcano that wanted to erupt, but never quite got there. Nobody ever really wants to kill himself. It's a cry for help that is never heard. People don't pick up on the signals, as they are too wrapped up in their own lives to notice. How anyone 'chooses to be depressed' is totally beyond me. All I've ever wanted to do is to live, and not just survive. So it is a flawed argument to assume that the thousands who have died by suicide had a choice about whether or not to end their life. The fact is that they obviously felt they didn't have any choice other than to carry out their equivalent of a lethal injection.

I remember how my mindset was the same each time I tried. I'd prepared myself for going to a place where I'd be at peace. I'd only ever felt such peace while I was asleep. That's how I was looking on it – as a long, never-ending, dream that would allow me to have the life I thought I ought to have. I wanted my death to be as quick and as painless as possible, although I thought that if I was going to a better place, it wouldn't matter if I had a few aches and pains – they'd soon disappear in my perfect orb. Hey... I might even have proper use of my left arm and leg. My belief that I would never to be hurt again was the best bit about it.

When I tried it for the first time, I cranked up the decibels on my CD player to hide what I was doing. On such a beautiful day, nobody would think twice about someone in the afternoon sunshine playing music that the whole street could hear. I sat in a brown '80s-style swivel chair that had linked me and my computer for so long. I couldn't believe some of the stuff racing through my head. My main angst was about what would Mum feel if my body flew past the window from the third floor bedroom. I'd written arrangements for how I wanted my funeral to go. I was going to be cremated, and I'd drawn up a list of people I didn't wish to attend, together with those I'd like to come – even though the chances of them doing so were slim. Yes, I'd invited all the people who had inspired me – mainly people who had been (or were still) in the public eye. I am very careful not to call them celebrities, because they were much more to me that that. What I wanted inscribed on my gravestone also filled a page of its own – no names of family or friends, just my favourite sayings. This was going to be *my* day, and even if I had to plan it before I went, then that's what it would take. Nobody would be able to spoil my send-off, because without anyone's knowledge, I had control.

My bed was next to the window, so I pretended to be enjoying the scorching heat by mouthing the words to songs as I looked up to the cloudless blue sky, waiting for the moment when I felt that I had the guts to go out with a bang. I flung my right leg over the side of the window, and then paused for another few minutes to see if this was what I really wanted. I grabbed hold for dear life to something hard, as knowing my luck, I'd lose my grip and fall to my death before deciding for certain whether or not it was going to make me happy.

I heard someone coming up the stairs, struggling to carry a heavy object. I wasn't hanging around to find out who, and what they were banging from wall to wall, and I was in the process of sliding my left leg to where my right was. My then best friend, Izzy, came in and slumped on the bed, exhausted after using so much energy lifting the hoover to the room for Mum. He asked what I was doing, and thinking fast, I told him that I was just trying to get a closer look at what material the roof was made of – checking to see if it was safe, as we didn't want any slates plummeting from a great height and killing someone as they passed. Whether he accepted my story or not, I don't know. In some respects you could say he saved my life, because his appearance had meant that I had to lie to cover my failed suicide attempt. Why he never said anything to Mum, I really don't know.

There'll be many that put their last pound on me being the least likely to want to take my own life. And if you said: 'Lee tried to kill himself at the weekend', they'd reply: 'Never! Why would he want to do that?'

People haven't seen me in the flat or in my bedroom at Mum's when I was fighting with myself, trying to figure out why I'm so different to everyone else. It hurts that others won't leave me to be the person I want to be – forever nagging, and alienating me even more from their clique. Not that you'd want to be a part of something like that, though – if you know what I mean. There's a certain mask I put on to suppress everything when I'm out and about, and it really annoys me that I feel I have to do that. If I were to live like a hermit, I'd go demented, and so to go to the pub and talk to people serves a purpose, even if it's not the right company.

I've been dying inside for as long as I can remember, and I don't know what to do to change things. Never quite feel as though I'm winning the race. Maybe one day it'll be different. Be happy at what you do have, rather than concentrating on what you don't have. Easy to say that if you haven't felt like me, and like lots of other folk. This kind of thing is all too commonly preached by those who have everything, and who have never heard of strife in their life.

My second go at ending it all was foiled, too. It was on a Sunday morning, and I had just finished my breakfast. I took my plate to the kitchen, and then went to take my epilepsy tablet. The lids on the medicine bottles are really annoying, and sometimes it could take me five minutes to open one up. I know they're supposed to protect kids from doing what I was about to do – except that they see the contents as sweets, and not as a killer drug. When you tip the bottle upside down, it's like a ripple effect when too many for their own good plunge towards the floor, as though they have a divine right to bounce about like some sort of Russian performing fleas. I despised having to bend and pick them up, so on that Sunday I thought the best way to avoid doing so was to swallow all of them and leave no trace of the pests. Didn't know whether it was enough to do any harm, although it seemed worth a try if nothing else. Of course, people in white coats might have me sectioned if Mum found out and told the doctor.

But then Craig walked in with his bowl. I was clutching the pills, and was just in the middle of chucking them down my throat, so maybe his entry wasn't such bad timing after all. He was about six, and I could see that his last memory of me, his big brother, shouldn't be of my collapsed body due to the effect of having taken an overdose. Yes, my conscience told me to turn my back to spill the tablets on to the chequered kitchen tablecloth.

When I think about it, my third bid seems pretty idiotic. On a Friday in Sixth Year, I could go home if I wanted, because I had a double free period in the afternoon. No point staying in a place that I loathed, if I could help it. Having been asked to leave all my subjects meant that my time there was a complete waste anyway. On that day, I signed the register to let the school know that I was accounted for – in case of a fire drill, or the real thing. Then I left, and I stepped onto the main road and closed my eyes. I had certainly not planned this course of action. I began to walk from the school to my house with my eyes shut, hoping that something would hit me. The reason for this was that, if I were likely to get tossed into the air and thrown to my death, I wouldn't have

49

much opportunity to get out of the way. Could you tell what direction a car or lorry was coming from, and how far away it was, without opening your eyes? Well, if you could, you're a better judge than I am, as I couldn't. I did sneak a peek once or twice to see if there was anyone watching a man who to them must have needed psychiatric help. I guess that because no one stopped me, people wanted me to get on with it, or there genuinely wasn't anybody about.

A third of a mile stood between the house and me, but in the time that it took me to walk it only one white transit van swerved past at great speed to sidestep a collision. The thought that someone had to react so fast to ensure his or her own safety scared me, as I was the cause for the diversion. Maybe I'm not one of the good ones that die young, I thought, though it didn't stop me trying a fourth time.

There are no words that can sum up how I feel when thinking of what I did, and this just goes to show how alone I felt. To want to decapitate yourself is something that none of us should have to go through. I couldn't find a knife or grater to slice some cheese for a sandwich. I usually came home for snack, as it was the only way to get peace to enjoy what I was eating. Some smart-arse would see what I was having, and either rib me or bore me rigid with the dangers of consuming what I was putting into my mouth. You know, like it was far healthier to have brown bread with no butter? I tried to hold the cheese still with my unreliable left elbow, while cutting what I needed with the largest knife from one of those sixty-piece sets folk always get as a wedding present yet rarely use. Anyway, I was worried about leaving the rest in the house – a disfigured block of cheese. Where most would laugh at sculpting their own vision of cheese with a six-pack, I wasn't laughing, and to make matters worse, I'd cut my finger! Blood trickled from a small nick in my finger, and this was enough for me to lose the rag.

I dropped to my knees and started to move the knife towards my neck. I was determined that this was how it was going to end, and I let the shiny stainless steel implement rest on my Adam's Apple, while deciding where I was hoping to burst an artery in order to bleed to death. I began to saw away, but either I didn't penetrate the skin adequately in order to set the wheels in motion, or someone really didn't want me to die. My hand was shaking so much I maybe wasn't as forceful as I thought I was. It felt as if I was being teased before somebody was about to take it upon themselves to finish the job. I was on my own, and if I did muck up before deciding for certain, then it was only I who was to blame.

I must be a cat with nine lives, because just then Marcus unexpectedly walked in to grab a seat to guzzle his dinner. I mirrored the look of horror in his eyes at seeing him catch me trying to cross to the next phase in life. I made the brainless excuse about recreating the moment in Highlander – the TV series – where the main character chops off the head of another immortal and gains all their powers. I wasn't acting like the hero, so he wouldn't have believed me. Marcus wasn't thick. A scrawny vegetable should have been the victim, not me. The following day he came round once more, to make sure I didn't try again.

My last stab was only a few years ago. I'd moved into my flat just months earlier. I'd had such a great night pub-crawling that it was quite painful returning to just four walls. I had nobody special to share my life with or tell of the evening just gone. It's one aspect of single life that I've adapted to, although for the first few weeks, having no one to say goodnight to, or make you a cup of tea the following morning, was very strange. I didn't see it as me being independent, but as me proving a point – that people really had no time to get to know me. Everyone who visited in the beginning stopped coming, and being on my own most of the time was something I didn't expect to be so difficult. There's a limit to how long you can play your music at full volume to try to forget how alone you are. Was it the fact that I hadn't, and still haven't, decorated the place that kept people away? Yes, I have a few nice material possessions like my guitar, my waterfall feature and my DVD player, but I've learned not to put importance on these things, as they are nothing compared with sweet fragile flesh and blood. Not perfect, but by God, man, alive – which is more than can be said for anything that doesn't breathe, and doesn't cry. Sorry, I've done it again... I quoted one of my favourite actors – Edward Woodward from Common As Muck when he played Nev. And it was based on a true story by William Ivory about the trials and tribulations of a group of dustbin men. Although it's not word for word, it's the essence of the speech that wraps up the twelve-part drama.

Never brag about what you have, as folk will only wag their finger in aversion. I love talking about Boon's guitar, how I got it, and what it's done long term. Some might think that I'm boasting about owning my favourite male solo artist's instrument, but they're wrong. Just bringing something interesting to the conversation that makes me stand out is what I've always wanted. I talk of him as though he's going to join me for a pint in five minutes, and I'm glad I haven't met the man behind the screen, because the image formed of him will not represent the actual person. People I've told think I'm in cloud cuckoo land, although I have documentation that proves I bought it from Boon for two hundred and fifty pounds. What more do they need? Why would I want to lie? I've no reason to. Is it because they can't relate to it? But that's not my fault, though.

Now back to my fifth suicide endeavour. Before heading to bed, I brushed my teeth, had a wee, took my tablet and then locked the door. I'd hurt my arm trying to shut myself away from the outside world, and lost the plot. Everything I did seemed to bug me, even the smallest things. 'Don't trouble trouble till trouble troubles you' I was once told. I've always made hard work of my worries – being too ashamed to say anything to anyone, as they have problems of their own and don't need me complicating matters. I know I didn't need to suffer in silence, but if it was my doing, and if I'm big enough and ugly enough to get myself into it, I should be big enough and ugly enough to get myself out of it. I went to the kitchen and took one of the specially-designed knives for cutting food. I went over to the door, planning to sit with my back to it. Like the first time, all sort of things were running through my mind, and I believe that only two things stopped me from piercing my stomach deeper than the initial graze I made when poking at my belly button. I really didn't know where I was going. That, and the thought of never hearing my favourite piece of music, watching my preferred TV programmes, eating the desired meal or seeing beloved Aberdeen again, made me hesitate.

Nobody has ever come back to tell us what it's like to be dead, or where we go. So before the Almighty One calls my number, someone had better let me in on the biggest kept secret since time began! The dream of meeting everyone that means something to me and living a heavenly life, is exactly that – just a dream. If I have the choice, I don't want to be reincarnated. Life isn't all peaches and cream, and not even returning as a vivacious, successful businesswoman that oozes sex-appeal is tempting. To know roughly what's in store for the next fifty or sixty years hardly inspires excitement. Though I don't believe we just get buried then eaten by maggots till all that's left is a skeleton. Life's too complicated for something like that to be waiting round the corner for us. People have been going to mediums and spiritualists for years, and even Mum has seen the good they do because she went to see one frequently when in Manchester. Okay, sceptics say that these people charge obscene amounts of money, but they get it right more often than not, and those who find comfort in connecting with the dead readily accept their terms. Of course, they can't be right all of the time, and some of the information they give might be a little inconsistent with what we already know ourselves. Yes, fraudsters identify vulnerable individuals, and then home in on these unlucky characters. But that happens in all lines of work these days – it's just the way society is. We're becoming too greedy for our own good, but to use the argument that these jazzed-up clairvoyants are taking many for a ride is wrong. The genuine ones out there do care about the people they talk to, and generally do a good job.

Open your mind to the possibility that our loved ones may not be as far away as we're meant to believe. Sometimes as I pot about the flat with Natalie and Rebekah (my sisters who did not make it beyond the foetal stage) on the brain, I'll see a butterfly sprinkled in lots of fluorescent colours rest on a picture frame. I wonder if this is one of the girls letting me know that she is close by. It's always annoyed me when others have said that they can't understand why I get so worked up about a couple of foetuses that were never given birth to. How can I not? Granted, they weren't here long enough to form individuality – though tell that to women who've carried one inside the womb for nearly nine months. They can't stop thinking about what could have been. They've felt the baby kick, and probably have hidden in their purses a scan photo that was taken at twelve weeks of gestation. It's impossible not be affected by that. Why do you think couples name the children they've lost? It's to deal with the grief, and to give importance to the life so tragically cut short. I hope to honour my sisters in some way, though I have yet to find a suitable homage. Getting a tattoo on my body or a chain with their names emblazoned has been done long ago and is not enough. I want to express my feelings in a manner that would also reflect my personality, and show that they're just as big a part of me as if they were in the same dimension as I am.

I don't think that the thoughts of suicide will ever go away. Since I've mulled over it the once, I think that when life gets tough I'm forever going to turn to thoughts of how others have succeeded beforehand. I probably won't ever try to do anything about it again, and the fact that I still have these thoughts isn't a worry. Do I really want to be like this for the remainder of my days? Of course not, but I'm trying to be as real as I possibly can when it comes to explaining the man you're all getting to know a little better the more you read on. That's why people's sticks and stones may break my bones, but names will never hurt me!

The Garden Party

It is said that there are two certainties when we join the human race – paying taxes, and death. To date, there have been eight whose arrival at the Gates of Heaven has had a profound effect on me. I've always wanted a sister – an older one rather than younger – so that when Mum leaves this dimension I can confide in big sis about my past, my disability, or anything to do with women, as she'd been there, seen it and got the T-shirt. Mum frequently brushed aside my questions of whether or not I had a sister I'd never met, or who died before I came along. She gave birth to me when she was twenty-two (she was twenty-three in the November, and I was born in the April), and I thought that, given our circumstances when I was young, it was quite possible that she could have had a miscarriage, complications at the birth, or even given the child up for adoption. Speculation can be misleading at its worst, and I needed to know either way. I found out for sure in crazy circumstances.

It was a Sunday evening and I'd been invited home for a rare Sunday roast. As I headed to Mum's along Langtongate (she lives at No.28, but used to reside in No.2) my eyes were attracted to something on the curb. There were two miniature Polaroid photos, face down. I, being sentimental when it comes to junk, decided to take the pictures to show Mum. They were of two babies. One was a boy, just a few months old, wrapped up in warm clothing and a blanket, sitting in a bouncing chair. The other was an angelic blonde girl, about two or three years old, standing in front of a radiator. After tea, Mum went upstairs to her bedroom for time out. Bewildered as to why she was so quiet, I went to see if she was okay. Playfully jumping on the bed, I asked if she was all right. Her reply was that she'd had a lot on her mind – mainly work at the bank. To change the subject and try to cheer her up, I brought the polaroid photos out. Of course, I also wanted to unmask the truth about my family. All the obvious questions and statements came from my mother. Where did I get them? Why did I bother picking them up? What was I going to do with them now I had them? What would people think of me raking on the floor as though I'd spotted a 1p or 2p coin and swiped it for good luck? I realised that she was kind of deflecting the conversation to suit the way she was feeling.

One of the main reasons for collecting the two photographs was that the girl reminded me of a younger version of Zoë, a friend of my then ten-year-old brother Craig. And you couldn't take one without the other, eh? They could be brother and sister for all I knew. It was plain to see that they'd come as a pair, and so should stay that way. Some beloved daddy had probably opened his wallet, and out they had fallen.

It later materialised that I indeed could have had two younger sisters, and this threw me into even more turmoil. Apparently, a couple of years after I was born, Mum was expecting a girl, but she had a terrible accident on the stairs, and Natalie didn't survive it. Two years on from this distressing punch to the gut, Paul joined the ancestry. Yet a further two years down the line, my mother found that she was pregnant with Rebekah. But, very sadly, she could not carry that pregnancy either. This explains why, when Paul came along, I had to choose either Paul or Carl if he was a boy, and Natalie or Rebekah if he was a girl. Natalie and Rebekah still drift in and out of my thoughts on a regular basis, and I think that they always will. I find myself constantly fantasising about what they would look like now, what their personalities might have been – especially when I see a gorgeous woman – not that you should be attracted to a female sibling.

Never did I anticipate that a footballer's loss of life would bother me that much, until he came from the team I supported. On June 26th 2003, Marc Vivien Foe, representing Cameroon in the Confederations Cup, collapsed in the centre circle after seventy-two minutes. South American opponents, Colombia, and the millions watching on TV wouldn't forsee the tragic circumstances set to send everyone affiliated with the game into mourning. As resuscitation procedures on the unconscious twenty-eight-year-old, winning his 62nd cap, were put into place, prayers could be heard by all of mankind, although forty-five minutes later, Foe, an ambassador for the African scene, was pronounced dead. Xavier Richard, through his second autopsy, revealed that no foul play or substance misuse was to blame, and Foe was deemed to have passed away due to natural causes. The initial testing had indicated nothing. Ironically, and surely not coincidentally, the semi-final tie was being played in Lyon, France.

Foe, on loan at Manchester City, my beloved blues, had been deliberating whether to leave his current employers – Lyon – and move to Lancashire to gain first team action. He'd scored nine goals in thirty-five appearances, and was starting to find his feet with some stunning performances, fast becoming a fan's favourite. Teammates from Lyon, Sidney Govou and Gregory Coupet, along with other members of the French and Turkish national sides, immaculately observed a minute's silence in their semi-final the following day. There was some doubt as to whether the tournament should see out its remaining fixtures, but with only the one semi-final and the final to go, sanctioning this would have been pointless. Pundits argued that carrying on is what Foe would have wanted.

The winning of this competition panned into perspective because of Foe's death, and anyone watching the French take their place against the 'Indomitable Lions' in the final, hoped, as it unfolded, that they wouldn't get caught up in the euphoria of going easy on their opposition. A large cardboard cut-out of Foe in his national colours was escorted onto the pitch by captain Rigobert Song and the entire squad. I was at my mum's house, and couldn't hold back the tears, even in the presence of her and my stepfather, Gordon.

The end ceremony kicked off what was going to be an emotional evening, whatever the result. France went on to lift the trophy, but the zenith for me was when Song put a loser's medal over one corner of the gigantic Foe picture. Yet again it set me off, and as France received the cup, they invited the Cameroon players onto the podium to loft the prize together. This was an unexpected moment to cherish. The unity shown must have made Foe looking down on it very proud.

Foe's appetite for the game was one that had spurred me into buying my first two Manchester City tops. It never entered my head that they'd cost nearly a hundred pounds, and what others thought quickly blew away like smoke. I had his name, though not the number twenty-three, pressed on to the back of the jerseys. Folk asked why I didn't get the number on the shirts, so I told them the club hadn't retired it for the fun of it. His name 'up in lights' along my shoulders was how I was going to rubberstamp my tribute to him. For me, he still has a role to play from the sky as the all-important twelfth man. When I wear the tops I feel a great sense of protection – as though the gentle giant is with me. Tons of people – mostly those not into football – have given me perplexing looks, before racking their brains to see if they should be scared of me!

Pronunciation is a part of the English language that has always interested me. Foe's name is pronounced 'foa' rather than 'foe', so it's not hard to see why many crash and burn when it comes to this subject. The most refreshing observation came by way of Alex Duncan, a guy I met at Robert Hay's, my local bookies. Alex forever states the obvious, although playing the senile old-age pensioner must come naturally to him after all these years. Being one of the regulars has its own perks, and as shaky starts go, my place in the asylum (Robert's words not mine) is guaranteed, now that I've done my apprenticeship in the run-down bus shelter – which is how I see the magical property. It has character when half-full that I've never felt when in a packed pub. Before I lose the story completely, I want to tell you that I walked into Robert's, ready to put on a bet. With Foe on my side, Alex noticed his name and went into a chorus of: 'Fe Fi Foe Fum, I smell the blood of an Englishman.'

I applauded the invention of Alex, because most would have sunk their teeth into all the Manc jokes. But not into Alex. He has the knack of being chief clown without actually realising it! So whenever I sport my true colours, I'm anticipating the reference to Jack and the Beanstalk, and, yes, it arrives on cue every time! Just as well I'm English too, or Alex's playful remark may have lost credence.

We'd want Foe on this side of the spiritual spectrum any day, although he'll be engraved in Manchester City history forever as the last player in a blue shirt to score at Maine Road. The last ever player to net there is attributed to Swede Matthew Svensson of Southampton in the Saint's 1-0 win. Foe's brace against Sunderland condemned them to imminent relegation after the 3-0 drubbing. His country's government awarded him full military honours and called for a day of remembrance to be held. All things considered, it really is like you've lost a member of your family. Marc had been an integral piece of the City jigsaw, and it's no wonder we fluctuated in the same style as a yo-yo – finishing just five points ahead of the relegation spots without him, as opposed to the dizzy heights of ninth when playing to his promise.

Disappearing into the sunset, the fourth shadow to have a bearing on how I see my own mortality is Ecky Hill, who stayed in the same block of flats as me. Grandad keeps telling everyone my bachelor pad resembles that of a Swiss villa from the exterior. The complex had its long-standing residents, and Ecky at No.3 was one of them. You could never have a conversation without mentioning Manchester United. Well, how great they were is about as far as it got! Ecky wouldn't hurt a fly, and I don't know a person who had a bad word to say about him. He always wanted me to meet his three kids – Duncan, Julie and Diane – from the Manchester area. I never did, until I bumped into Duncan when vying for a urinal in the White Swan toilets on the first anniversary of Ecky's death.

Crafty Bob, Ecky's best mate for almost forty years, had urged me to go and see him before he left for the other side. Doctors had given Ecky just a matter of weeks to live, after diagnosing him with cancer of the pancreas. I'll always remember seeing Ecky on the Thursday before he died in hospital on the Tuesday of the following week. How do I remember? I had hijacked his edition of the Berwickshire News as a souvenir. There were two things that made me face the inevitable sooner rather than later. One was the amount of weight he'd shed, and the other was the colour of his skin. Alcohol was to be his killer, and the smeared shade of yellow that littered his body brings a tear to my eye.

Thinking about his demise, I'm glad I said goodbye, as something inside racks you with guilt if you don't – almost as if you've served the deceased a degree of disloyalty. His funeral on the Friday of the same week was hailed as one of the best ever for the sheer numbers that turned up to pay their last respects. I didn't go, knowing that I'd crack under the strain of what the day would entail. Instead, I chanced going to the cemetery when I thought everyone had gone home. I actually entered the holy realm as the final flock of mourners were making their exit. I walked between the hundreds of gravestones, carefully avoiding stepping on any of the other friendly ghosts. That thought took my mind off meeting with death's door. When I reached his final resting place, a hefty-looking undertaker with glasses was lumping soil onto Ecky's coffin. On bended knee, I watched from a few yards away, while the man patted every ounce of earth with a spade until no part of the wooden box could be seen. Then he used all the bouquets of flowers to arrange a pretty rockery. The sight of a delivery van and heavy goods vehicle on the road in and out of Duns while this commemoration was in progress pointed a finger to the fact that life goes on whether we want it to or not.

Epitaphs are meant to symbolise a person's character in some way, and Ecky's couldn't have been chosen any better. 'His life a beautiful memory, his absence a silent grief.' Rain lashed down, soaking me to the bone, and I swithered about whether to stay and see Ecky get the perfect send-off. There was no contest!

When you meet someone's relative at the wake, they usually have a story to tell of the departed. Mine features another neighbour of ours, Bob Ramage, married to Ina, and both living in No.1. I'd ordered some 'Level 42' merchandise, and was paying for it by cheque through the post. I managed to write the address of Mark King on the envelope, but mucked it up when trying to seal it with a stamp. Thank God for the adhesive alternative! Anyway, as I went to search for someone to help me in my quest to finish the job and get it off before the last pick-up, I found Ecky and Bob deep in discussion at the bottom of the stairs leading to numbers three, four and five. Feeling rather ashamed, I interrupted their private chat to ask for a little assistance. Ecky thought it would be a good idea to stick the back together with some sellotape. So Bob went inside his flat to gather a pair of scissors and a roll that was almost finished. This was to guarantee no mishaps on its journey to the Isle of Wight.

I never anticipated that we'd still be it at half an hour later. With the sellotape on its last legs, Bob really tested Ecky's patience. All Ecky wanted to do was to snip the strip himself, yet Bob had ideas of his own. He thought that I should hold the envelope closed, while Bob held the sellotape and Ecky cut two strands to add the finishing touches to the masterpiece we were concocting. Anyone who might have happened to earwig as they trotted past must have thought what a bunch of plonkers we were. To see three grown men take so much pride in what they were doing, and still make a hash of it, would have won us two hundred and fifty pounds on You've Been Framed. Precision was never the strong point!

One afternoon I spontaneously went to Sunflowers, the local florists, and bought some red and white carnations to place on Ecky's grave. On leaving the shop, a woman I knew – Lynne MacVicar – asked who the lucky lady was. I never flinched before spouting a load of bull about them being for my mother. I didn't want someone snooping into my business, especially in a town as transparent as Duns.

It was quite surreal two days after Ecky's death, when in the White Swan an old mate of mine, Neil, and I toasted to the end of one life and the beginning of another.

In April/May 2001, I was involved in an Internet auction for Boon Gould of Level 42's Reno Yellow Les Paul Hoyer guitar. I wasn't the highest bidder, but at the end of thirty-one days, I became the owner of a piece of British Pop memorabilia. Gave the man seven hundred and fifty pounds, but there is a twist in the tail, so stay tuned!

The thing I didn't expect after buying the instrument was that writing about the arrival of the guitar at my flat for its retirement should result in frequent e-mail correspondence for nearly three years with my musical idol.

During this time, I learned of the many 'ins and outs' of Rowland Charles Gould born March 4th 1955 on the Isle of Wight. Media tittle-tattle can be scandalous when it comes to announcing the breakup of a group, and Level 42's separation was covered with a few inaccuracies. It was these kinds of admission which became the basis of our 'You've Got Mail' shenanigans.

In one message, he revealed that he was going to be a father by his partner Moira. I felt very privileged that he would entrust me not to leak this fabulous news to fellow digesters on the Net. They would get to know when Boon saw fit, and pictures were posted on his website a few months after the wee boy's birth. Solomon Ulysses Gould was born on Thursday 13th June 2002, and on the Friday, during happy hour, we raised flutes, or rather a can of Coke and pint of Guinness to Ecky and Solly!

If there's one thing Ecky's death taught me, it's to live every day as though it's your last and that it really is time you never put off till tomorrow what you can do today. You only ever seem to miss people when they're gone, and one of my Quiz team members didn't have the most dignified or worthy passing.

I'd known Jessie Atkins for almost six years, through her working at the White Swan. She had one of those infectious laughs, behind which hid her encyclopaedic brain. Whatever she didn't know, she made up with her zany wit. I think calling her everyone's maternal grandmother is selling Jess short – but it is probably true, nonetheless.

I was in the Quiz team from the very beginning, and witnessed all the personnel reshuffling. When I first joined, there was Jess, my auntie Susan, Tim Aubery, Maurice Cook and Joe McNally. This was a taste of what was to become the norm every fortnight for the next six years. I felt 'a part of something special', and as my comrades fell by the wayside, who was there, holding up the rear for reinforcements to arrive? It was none other than Jess. She was the backbone of the regiment.

The hardest question was what we were going to call ourselves, and for a while we were somebody different each week. Joe and Maurice, for reasons only known to them, were injured on the battlefield and left to fly home to their families. Excuse me, I've gone with the military theme and must run with it now. That still left Jess, Tim, myself and Susan to defend the barricades before bringing in new blood. Tracy, Jess' daughter, and her ex-partner, David Murray, would give us a more settled side that brought balance to our strategic movement. We each had our specialist round now. Mine was Sport, Susan's was Entertainment, Dave's was Music, Tracy's was Newspapers, and Jess and Tim had a bit of everything, and ruled the roost on General Knowledge.

For ages, we'd either win the Quiz hands down or finish second. Never being out of the top two was good to begin with, until other teams got fed up. Numbers tumbled to an all-time low, and although still there in body, I don't believe we're all there in spirit anymore. At its worst, there we were, with our arch enemies, the Fuzzy Ducks, in a University Challenge-style dual. Crumbling wasn't in our nature, but after Tim stopped coming, we lost the fun and got too serious. Getting beat, and beat comprehensively, was a feeling we weren't used to, and we were asked whether we were just in it for the glory or because we enjoyed each other's company regardless of whether we won or lost.

I'm not one you can pull the wool over easily, but my teammates said that the Quiz Master geared it up for the Fuzzy Ducks – which is ludicrous to suggest, especially as you can't prove it. So, if we win now, it's a bigger buzz than when we were the smart arses – and nobody likes one of them!

Evolution is pivotal if you want to succeed, and just meeting up every two weeks should have been enough to keep us together. I guess being there for Jess' sake just wasn't in our minds. Dave was given compassionate leave, never to return after splitting with Tracy, while Susan had been disengaging on and off whenever it suited her, with Tim's lassie understandably more important to him than we were. James Lough, one of the funniest men I've ever met, and Kenny Whitecross, a mine of useless information, were then recruited to the All Saints Army.

That used to be our permanent title until Jess passed over. Her sudden death, following a seventeen-day bedside vigil, has hit us all in different capacities. One minute she was there, and the next she was gone.

Unlike in the case of Ecky, after hearing of Jess' fall from grace, I decided I wanted to remember her as I last saw her, so never went to see her at the Borders General Hospital, Melrose. I did not want to see her wired up to bleeping machines and tubes that made a mockery of a once-respected pillar of the community. Doctors said after almost ten days that she had a chest infection. Then a few hours down the line, she suffered a minor stroke and was being kept alive by a ventilator and a strong heart.

Less than a week later Tracy, sisters Carol, Claire and Dawn, along with husband Bill, made the gut-wrenching decision to switch off her ventilator. I remember where I was when I was given the tearful news. Sarah Jane Lindsay on shift at the Swan came over to whisper what we'd expected from the moment she entered the BGH. Hasn't really sunk in for me yet. No doubt Jess has made friends with Ecky, Mr Foe, Natalie, Rebekah and a school pal, Stuart Bowden – who I'll tell of very soon – in looking over me.

When the funeral came, I did exactly what I'd done with Ecky – skipped the church service and went straight to the graveyard when I thought no one would be there. This time the sun was shining from here to Edrom (sorry, a saying that Robert has in the bookies), and I thought it was kind of poignant because I'd never seen Jess without a beaming smile. Again I sat on the grass till every grain of muck had been levelled out, giving Jess a burial to be proud of. Tears streamed off my chin onto my Filthy Monkey T-shirt, so to anyone passing it might have looked as though I'd dribbled like a newborn baby. It didn't matter as I walked the short distance to Ecky's stone to tell him that a familiar face had moved in round the block! I'm one for doing crazy things like that.

If there's only one memory I was to keep about Jess, it's when she answered a sports question in the Quiz which gave us a maximum ten out of ten – one of the very few we've had in our time. We were quietly confident of eight or nine, but found the winner of the 1970 derby a tough nut to crack. None of the teams had the rabbit up the sleeve, so Willie gave us all a clue. When it mattered most, Jess would always come up with the perfect punch. Writing 'Nijinsky' on a note pad, it was easy as ABC 123, if you were to see Jess light up the Empire State

Building with the twinkle in her eyes. So when Willie revealed the answers and Nijinsky was right, Jess' reaction was uncharacteristic for a Thursday night. The clenched fist thrown in the air – a sign that she demanded nothing but the best when we came out to pit our wits against what Duns had to offer in opposition.

Even from her fluffy white cloud, Jess still gets others in the living gamut to look after me. One night, whilst out at the pub, her granddaughter, Teri, asked how I was. A lot of the time I'm 'on my own' when socialising. I don't particularly like it, but can't mope about at home. Just have to get on with it. Okay, some people say 'you're a loner', and they may be right to a point. However, what is not taken into account is that I may actually prefer to be a free spirit and just do my own thing.

I'm way too deep for most of the people I've met in Duns, and yes, you do have to be thick-skinned when they alienate you because you're different. I've heard, although, yes, it's not gospel, that there are a lot of folk who think quite highly of me. Well, I'll believe it when I see it. I'm not one for expecting them to come and pat me on the back and tell me what a swell guy I am – that kind of thing just never happens. What may change my mind is when people stop judging me, and try to get to know the 'proper Lee' whom none of them has ever seen. For whatever reason, too many dismiss me before they've even spoken a word – probably because I'm right in your face, trying to win you over, before the negativity sets in.

I must say that I do get on with people from outside the town more than I do with people from Duns. It seems to me that inhabitants of this town aren't interested in the lives of everyone around them. Maybe they only came here to switch off!

Anyway, on this night, Terri wanted to know if I was all right. I wasn't feeling out of sorts or anything, although it was nice to know that someone was concerned. After I'd given Terri my answer, she said that all she was doing was carrying out a family tradition. This confused me somewhat. It turned out from Terri's talk that Jess used to worry about me between Quiz night on a Thursday to the following Tuesday, when she usually saw me on her first shift of the week. I don't know what she thought was going to happen to me. Fall in love perhaps? Then, when her health deteriorated, she gave up some of her hours, and so there was a longer interval between seeing each other.

It's bizarre how we only get to know these things when people have been taken from us. If people just communicated with one another while we were able to make it count, this world would be such a better place.

Next, Stuart Bowden is promoted to left-hand guardian angel. I sat beside him in Standard Grade Maths for two years, although like most of the Chirnside posse, he wasn't a mate. If anything, on the outside he seemed the 'unpopular rascal' who sadly lost his life after a night on the tiles.

In the summer of 1997, along with three others, Stuart was involved in a car crash – he being the odd soul to perish. When emergency services arrived on the scene, it was found that he'd died instantly from a broken neck. There were no scratches or bruises – nothing on his body to show he'd ever been in the carnage between Chirnside and Allanton.

One of the clearest apparitions I have of Stuart at school is that when he'd finished an exercise, everyone would know about it! This showboating usually ended in Mr Stormin' Norman Anderson telling Stuart off for being too noisy and demonstrative.

However, if it so happened that he got stuck with his work, Stuart had no hesitation in peeking over your shoulder to see what you had written. Turn the tables, and Stuart would have every utensil of his pencilcase packed away so as not to give you his answers. Seems irrelevant how annoying that was, after everything that's happened since.

A parent's nightmare has always been outliving their children. Nature taking an out-of-the-blue zigzag detour is something you'll never get over. What with Stuart's sudden death shortly after leaving the school, I sometimes feel that I'm kind of selfish really, considering I made attempts to kill myself half a dozen times in my teens. Both, and not just one of us, should be enjoying life to the max at such a tender age.

There are some classmates who either love school reunions or avoid them completely. Stuart's not even going to get that choice – which is why I move rapidly to the next spirit guide, Judy, Ed's mum. Ed was one of my best mates, and his mum looked after my brothers and me when staying with us following the breakdown of her marriage to Ed's dad, James. They (Judy, Ed, and his two sisters, Ruth and Alice) eventually got their own house in the town, before emigrating again about an hour down the coast a few months later.

It's claimed that it takes two for a friendship to survive long distance. That's why I'm happy to admit my share of the blame in not keeping in contact. I should have made more of an effort, seeing as Judy visited me in my new flat shortly after I moved in. I promised to repay the compliment, and venture outside my comfort zone, though never did. I didn't know she was on her last legs until two days before she died.

I'd been trying to get a hold of Ed to see if he'd play in a charity football match for me, but I only got his sister Ruth, who informed me that her brother had become a little detached from the immediate family on finding out that his mum had just a few months to live, as she had been diagnosed with an untreatable form of cancer.

Really expecting time to arrange some kind of final meeting with Judy, there was utter disbelief on hearing of her death two days after the conversation with Ruth – barely five weeks into the battle with a killer disease. I wasn't briefed when it came to the funeral so couldn't go, and I won't chastise any of the kids for this. I was probably the least thing on their minds – what with losing their mother so close to Christmas. I just thank my lucky stars that I still have mine at twenty-six.

It's not just one pal who's lost a parent so young. My other friend, Joe, lost his father when he was almost sixteen, and this is something that brings me nicely to the last person boarding the flying red carpet. With the grandma on my mum's side of the family tree, there's a deeper significance.

I never got to meet Mrs Lillian Horton, as she was called, because she too was taken away from us so early in life. I couldn't understand why Mum always got upset on Christmas Eve each year, until it was revealed that Grandma, at the tender age of twenty-eight, lost a fight with bronchitis that very day in 1961. Yes, Granddad remarried, though because I live in an entirely different part of the UK, we (my brothers Paul, Craig, and I) have hardly had a chance to strike up a bond with our elders – the kind of people that so many get a great deal out of. However, there is some connection of sorts with his first wife.

My mum is a big believer of life after death, and I want to tell you about a particular reading that she once got from a medium. On the tape, which this spiritual meeting recorded, there's a reference to each of her three children. They talk of the eldest as 'one who has both emotional and physical difficulties, none of which is his fault'. Kind of cool, don't you think, that there's someone who agrees with me on one or two issues, even if I can't introduce them to anybody! Also, when Mum was looking for a way out of her relationship with my father, it seems that she was given a sign to go that was given to her by Grandma via another practising psychic. Supposedly, there was a woman clutching the hands of two small boys with her head bowed coming forward to pass on a message. This is obviously my brother Paul and I being led away in the presence of our grandmother. How do we know this? She writes her name in the dust on a table where a vase of pink and white tulips sit. The flowers (my grandma's favourite) validate the individual who shares what puts many minds at ease.

Some might say that Lilly did great good by this intervention, so here's praying that she manages in time to restore order and save another two lives. Would you believe me if I said Ecky and Marc are at loggerheads about which side of the city – the red or the blue side – has the best football team? No? Well do, because it's all going on at the 'Garden Party' hosted by the Big Man Upstairs Himself!

The Chocolate Wonder

Characters. Every town has one or two – people who epitomise what life's all about. Enjoyment. As an old man with a nip in one hand and a half pint in the other once said to me: 'We're here for a good time, son, not a long time.'

I first met Harry Brown about two years ago. I could relate to this legend from the moment we met. I much preferred to have his company than the folk I'd wasted the last few months with. His presence humbly brought a certain sense of closure to my own problems. He seemed to cope so much better than I ever did. Even after learning of his condition – spina bifida – it took me a while to stop worrying about how sore it would be if he fell. I'd never seen him stumble, so why was I fretting? Maybe he wasn't scared of asking for help if there came a time when he did end up on his bottom.

I'd always found it embarrassing and patronising when seeking assistance. Then, when I was nineteen, I dropped my lunch on the floor in a well-known fast-food franchise – not once, which was bad enough, but twice. The incident made me realise that, stubborn as I am, there will always be things I need to get others to do – like cutting my right-hand fingernails.

Amazingly, though probably not coincidentally, whenever our paths cross, without fail Harry raises a smile on my face. I'm not bothered about people's reactions when seeing us together. I think you're a special person if you have the ability to cheer someone up without trying. Don't you just hate it when one before their time can make something look so ridiculously easy?

Yeah, we are all capable of great things, but there are those who stand out from the crowd. Guess there has to be somebody who takes over my mantle, eh? However, I'm sure Harry's been here before. I can just tell. Don't ask me to explain. That's not me being big-headed. I appreciate everything around me.

One day, I'll find whatever it is I've been put on Earth for. Until that point, I'll try and savour the happy days. Such days are few and far between for most. People often ask if I think I'd be a different person without the disability. Of course I would. Frightens me to think I could have been the stereotypical chauvinistic pig that resembles such a large proportion of my age bracket. Either that or a total ned. Don't know which is worse. Okay, I accept we're not all like that. I do however love myself as the person I am.

An older lady told me recently: 'You're a very articulate, highly intelligent lad for your age.' I laughed at her for the wicked compliment she gave. Didn't, and still don't, know how to accept these words which praised me.

That's why I can't fathom the bond I've carved with Harry. Nothing is ever asked of the other. All friendships should be the same. Yes, there are instances where, because of his mood, the frustration shines through and restlessness creeps in. This hopefully isn't held against him. Must be difficult for his family at times, especially when meeting a brick wall head on. It's the reason why I love the bloke to bits and will try my best to lend a hand if needed. Got lots of resolve. He's already given me a sign of how he sees us...

Whilst minding my own business walking across Market Square, I heard someone shouting my name. Like a prize idiot, I did a 360-degree spin numerous times to locate the individual, pleased to have found a friendly face (or highlighting the fact that the voices in my head were doing overtime). I crouched down so that Harry could share the same eye level, and the man himself trundled over to see me from his spot on the bench beside his mum. As Harry gave me a hug then a kiss on the lips saying that he loved me, it was obvious that chocolate ice cream had been on the menu.

Those words, and the moment itself, will remain in my thoughts for a very long time. Not the sort of thing you forget in a hurry. It had been as though time froze so that someone could catch us for posterity on camera in that split second. Over in a flash. Sorry for the pun. I'm forever doing that.

Don't get me wrong. It's not that I've never before been touched by someone's unfortunate circumstances. I've just never encountered the close understanding with the disadvantaged before. Despise using words like that to describe Harry – or anybody for that matter. Sadly, it's the way in which society pigeon-holes his kind. Must stop that. Sounding more like an ignorant twat the longer I talk about the majority's view. It's as if Harry and Co. don't have a mind of their own to express what they're thinking.

It'll be interesting to see exactly how and what Harry does with himself over the next decade or so. Will he achieve his ultimate goal – to be a part of the most famous puppets in small-screen animation? Only time will tell. What I will say is I'll make sure that wherever I am in the world, I'll stay in touch.

If my writing career takes off, there are hardly any guarantees that I'll be in Duns at all. I know that's rather presumptuous, but I have to leave no stone unturned. The picture of us together, taken in my local, will go everywhere with me. He's the kind of dude you just wanna rave about to everyone you meet! There was once an occasion where he danced to a tune on the jukebox with his friends, Leah, Tai and Jordan, and stole the show. Coolness personified without doubt – he had me in stitches. Believe the gang will only enhance their open-mindedness by having Harry as a mate. I'm in no position to judge anyone in a better or worse state than mine. So neither should Harry's pals. Comes with the territory, and I could go on about this wonder-kid till the crack of dawn, but won't enlarge his ego. Not good for him because there'll come a time when he has to learn from his mistakes like we all have to. If the truth be known, the guy has given me the impetus to explore a path in working with youngsters – something which many have said I would thrive on. The recognition I get from the new generation is a tremendous boost to my confidence. Guess there is a buzz when interacting with someone who's made the effort to come talk to you just because they know your nickname from school.

'Kick his ass, SeaBass!' Great line isn't it? Discovering my possible vocation in life is down to only one fella. I'll not insult your intelligence by giving you a few clues. You've got it already. Yep, the newest addition to the Tracey Island clan: Protector of Thunderbird No.6 – Harry Brown himself! Not bad going for a five-year-old, eh?

Train of Thoughts

I've always thought that trains are a great place to meet people – that's if you're not one of those unsociable gits who sits looking out of the window with an MP3 player whisking the listener off to another planet, or who buries their head in a book that reveals an interesting insight into the reader's literary taste! Yes, it depends on the mood we find ourselves in as to whether we're the life and soul of the party or are happy enough just being a tiny segment of the pass-the-parcel circle. However, many a time I've felt like a tool, though not before trying to detect people to chat to after wading through numerous carriages. Unfortunately, it's hard to integrate if you've failed to join the excitement from the start of a journey – especially if asking to take the last pew at the across-the-aisle eight-seater seminar, where the banter has been flowing just as much as the drink! Nevertheless, when push comes to shove, those thespians I have clicked with by no means leave me. This is why I want to tell you about Urchin – a guy that purposely altered the way I looked at myself forever.

I remember watching an interview on TV with Beck, who said that the thing he liked most about touring was seeing something different each morning from the many hotel rooms he had slept in. This idea thrust me into spending the afternoon somewhere else, so off to the big metropolis I went one mild autumn day. I ended up buying five CDs in HMV and Virgin – as I repeatedly do when in the close proximity of my nearest megastores. It's well worth the hour's travel for choice alone, as the local retailers stock absolute tosh if allowed an opinion on the matter. Just because something's in the charts and popular, it doesn't necessarily mean it's good. The indoctrinated types seldom end up hearing lots of the great sounds of our time, and that is why I'd set myself a challenge to broaden the collection I had. It wasn't so much that I was getting bored by what I was listening to, but rather that I needed a little extra inspiration from other artists.

Ever since I'd seen Thea Gilmore on Jools Holland there'd been a desire in me to be exposed to further solo females. The catches were that they had to have a connection to me (like the first girl I formed a crush on might have been called Sarah), and I wasn't to have heard of them before, and their Christian names had to start with each letter of the alphabet! Over a year later I'm still trying to complete the operation, but lately it's dropped down the pecking order as I've had jobs to do, so it's not a surprise that my perfect woman hasn't surfaced.

Anyway, as I settled into my surroundings on the train, ready to go home, I began to rip up the outer packaging to throw into the bin. This was to save a few minutes once I was back at my flat. Then a fella asked if anyone was sitting in the three empty spaces, to which I replied that he should be my guest. His voyage was longer than mine (heading for Leeds), but I'm glad I gave Urchin the importance everybody deserves. I could have easily ignored the guy after he'd shown curiosity in what harmonies and melodies I'd acquired. Put it this way, the debate made my chunk of the ride go a lot quicker. What Urchin couldn't understand was why so many of us focus for acceptance and value upon the VIPs of the celebrity circuit and the lavish unfulfilling existences they lead. He thought that everyone was his or her own superstar.

If only we tried looking to ourselves for the answers as to how we can make best of why we are here in the first place, and stopped comparing our quandaries with those of others, then life would be so much easier. Society has coiled this problem for making people feel that they have to compete with the rich and famous just to be classed as a 'somebody'. Achievement can be defined in all sorts of ways – whether it's passing your driving test at the 42nd attempt or being the owner of a chain of fancy restaurants. Everything in this world should be deemed significant, although it never is.

I will admit that when Urchin first loomed towards me I was a bit apprehensive, especially in light of the recent terrorist bombings in and around the UK. But I learned that day how fundamental it is not to tarnish everyone with the same brush. And yes, he did have a fluency in the English language, so was probably born here, although he preserved his physical Asian outer shell. It's kind of sickening to have to make tracks all too soon if I've had a pleasant discussion with someone.

An ultimate goal of mine is to be film-maker who pioneers a believable thought-provoking tale about five strangers that meet on a sleeper and suffer a nightmare passage. I love the possible dynamics of it all. For starters, we need to know why each person has made the trip.

And there's the scope to give the characters whatever personalities you invent. The fact that nobody but those on board know about what went on after they've parted is another slant I'd take pleasure in examining. Suspense created by background composition is an element of film that intrigues too. Plummeting into the dark side of the things we do to live through testing contexts literally scares the living daylights out of me. A day when knowledge isn't harvested, or efforts made to do something that frightens the spirit, is a day wasted – if memory serves me right? Pictured in my head are the holy performers I'd love to be acting as the main creatures. I won't reveal who they are, as it's a must to keep it secret.

I hope that wheels are in motion that are designed to take the giant strides that'll move me onto the next level of my development as a human being, and that I'll see something of that happening in the not-so-far distant future. Maybe Urchin's got things sussed. Do I owe it to myself or to the man himself when seeing my potential? And where am I as things stand now? Well, being told that you have the face of Coldplay's squeaky-clean Chris Martin is pretty hilarious, and to boot that you have an arrogant accent like Oasis' nutcase Liam Gallagher is even funnier. (I originate from the same city as Liam, so we're bound to sound similar.) Being told that my skills resemble those of R.E.M.'s enigmatic Michael Stipe's knack of song writing is flattery I'm not used to either. And to top it all off, owning a Les Paul Hoyer guitar – which was once unsung Boon Gould's of Level 42 – is just the icing on the cake. Is my dress sense really like that of the virtuoso Ludwig van Beethoven? As nobody's around to argue otherwise, I'll just go with that. Having any of my peculiar mannerisms likened unto those of the wacky Mark Berry aka 'Bez' of The Happy Mondays, and bullet-proof drive of Tenacious D's warm-hearted Jack Black, could never be an unwelcome shock to the system. Sorry, my friends, the knock at the dressing-room door lets me know I've five minutes before I'm due on stage, and punctuality is a quality that I think highly of in people.

My turn has been a long time pending, so I'll enjoy riding on the crest of a wave that takes us on a mind-boggling jaunt of tunnels and bends. I'm a man whose life of Riley is, with a bit of luck, about to commence. I will ensure that welcome intrusion from the press is an aspect of the business that doesn't ruin what I experience when eventually realising my dream of becoming a critically-acclaimed author.

Until I have my first bestseller on the shelves, the pop career will have to do! This sudden mini-triumph is for the legions that told me I couldn't do it. Every now and then we have to do things that we haven't planned in order to get what we yearn for. The reservations of some have spurred me on in my mission to prove that the self-confidence I have, in spite of my afflictions, has never been a misplaced hallucination. Damn, I've forgotten the words to the opening track! It's a matter of urgency that I hone the raw flair a bit further, eh? Knowing that one is the 'World's First Most Definitive Rock and Roll Superstar' who is wowing the fans is a thankless task. Guess there's no rest for the wicked, then. See you later folks – I've a show to put on!

Hat-Trick

Will people be talking about me when I'm gone? I doubt it. They don't even talk about me while I'm here! As it goes, first impressions seem to be everything – so for anybody to be able to recognise and embrace what I'm really like is well-nigh impossible, as the herd have yet to see the best of me. If they do get to watch my true intrinsic worth, the passionate bloke behind it all is the first thing I hope they'd pick up on. Where do I get this from? I'm not quite sure, because it's something that doesn't run in the family. Connecting with those I have no choice in being related to has been a constant brawl. At times in the past, I've wondered whether I was cradle-snatched in the hospital and swapped at birth. Several don't give my uncertainties the importance they warrant. I've yet to make it in the industry, as I've no decent support network. I know not everyone will welcome everything anyone puts on paper, but to rebuff a work of fiction without any valid assessment is fairly puerile. From what I'm told, anyone can write a book, so I'm not that extraordinary. I have enough power of forgiveness and doggedness never to let bastards grind me down, and this has always ensured that I stay one step ahead of the cynics.

Following Aberdeen Football Club is my chief hobby, and it was whilst taking in three quick-fire away games in March 2007 that I finally realised this nonconformist life of mine is just as precious as the next. Judging a person on how he gets money to live, or how little significance he places on physical appearance, is something I've grappled with since I started school. Personally, I don't give two hoots about whether you come from a wealthy background or sleep rough on the streets, as long as you treat me the way you want to be treated yourself. Remember, manners cost you nothing. Mum's told me that if anybody has difficulty with my income, I've to tell them it's hers, my brother's and grandfather's tax that pays for me, not theirs. I'd never thought of it like that before. I get quite disturbed when sections of the community assume that I'm a bandit who sponges off the State. My writing has always been important to me, because it's usually how I make sense of the discontentment that infests my brain, and I'm trying to pass on a message to the whole of humanity that this existence could be a lot better for ourselves if we only tried a bit more with others.

The first part of the following successful trilogy was set in Falkirk, at a ground I'd never been to. I had a couple of extra hours in bed, as on her way to do the monthly shopping, Mum dropped me off in the middle of Berwick-upon-Tweed thirty minutes before my train departed for Edinburgh Waverley. Instead of having to catch a bus – using my free pass – the lift meant little hanging around. Using public transport would not have been an issue for me, as I'd thought about killing time by going for a proper English breakfast in a café near to the station – my usual matchday routine. Leaving on an empty stomach isn't wise for a pastime that seems to take up all of the weekend – Sunday being an opportunity to recharge your batteries. To get the most out of my appointments with the Dons, I use energy levels that I hardly believed existed. The day includes much more than the game itself. Friends you meet along the way and the things that happen to you before, during and after a game are sometimes just as memorable, especially if your heroes have been well and truly stuffed. In an effort to make the day feel as if it's been worthwhile, I always take the whole picture into account.

I remember my annoyance at not being able to have a conversation with a Polish man I sat beside instead of joining a hen party full of gorgeous girls where I might have found a soulmate! Later, there was the fear that I'd miss my rail link to the Central Belt if I didn't find the right platform quickly enough – even if there were twenty minutes to spare. Andrew, a university student I'd bumped into, steadied the ship and entertained me with his plans to meet up with a few mates who had chosen to do their thing at the Stirling campus. Prior to the doors opening to let us on, I saw from a distance a guy called Alex Dooley, who used to be in my year at the High School. I shouted to grab his attention, but he obviously never heard me, and I saw that he was chaperoning a beautiful young lady to her train. I'd seen him once or twice since we'd finished at the B.H.S., but I'd hardly expected to see the chap in these circumstances. And, of course, I like to get as far away from Duns as possible – not bring it with me! I discovered that another fella, who was sitting across the aisle studying the coupon, happened to have a grandmother with the surname Sheppard, and who had been brought up in Duns. This made me chuckle. I back the 'sheepshaggers' through thick and thin – so it had to be an omen. I arrived at Grahamston forty minutes down the line, the man with the coupon gave me directions to the stadium, and I left him to fend for himself on the remainder of his trip. The two-carriage service terminated at Dunblane. That place frightened me a little – what with being so close to the scene of Thomas Hamilton's pointless execution of sixteen defenceless pupils and their teacher in March 1996.

A reason to look forward to the game was that I'd get to watch Danish talisman Peter Schmeichel's son, Kasper, follow in his father's footsteps by playing in goal for the opposition. If he was even half as good as his dad, I knew we'd be hard pressed to score one past him, never mind a barrel load. Our best bet was to emphasise his inexperience at any given break of the ball. Liam Craig, a lad who had played against my brother in the local junior ranks, had also stepped up to the demands of the SPL after waving goodbye to Ipswich Town. It was going to be a fascinating battle of wits. You knew that the teenager would make the big stage sooner rather than later – trying to hamper your team's aspirations of European qualification with a touch of silkiness, nurtured by Trinidadian architect, Russell Latapy. (Started on the bench, but gaffer John Hughes kept the left-sided utility player wrapped in cotton wool, ready for a game he may have more impact on.)

When I went to buy the programme, I found that the boy selling them didn't have change of a tenner, and this meant that I had to head towards the club shop, where I got in tow with a steward whose uncle had lived in Whitsome – a small hamlet less than ten miles out of Duns – donkey's years ago. Small world, ain't it? I spoke to a nutty gentleman while I was munching on my hamburger and Mars Bar and drinking a large Coke. All that had cost me three pounds thirty. He thought that I ought to be pleased with myself for having the guts to come to the football on my own, knowing that I would have to face some frustrations – like carrying my drink from the counter to my seat without spilling it. Whilst guzzling my juice and chatting with the imposter pretending to be ex-Falkirk, ex-Dundee United, then Queen of the South boss Ian McCall, I avoided this worry becoming a reality. My train fare had cost twenty-two pounds and forty pence with the admission costing a further nineteen pounds, and then there was the ridiculous price of two pounds fifty for the programme. The game had better be worth it, I said to myself.

To say we mugged 'The Bairns' is an understatement, if there ever was one. Gary Dempsey, on the verge of signing for League One side Yeovil Town, reacted quickest to a half-cleared Barry Nicholson corner to drive home a rasping volley from the edge of the 18-yard box on sixteen minutes. I couldn't explain why the Red Coats Brigade had a holiday camp feel to it. This was something that depressed me. When Ricky Foster doubled our lead with a simple tap-in from a Darren Mackie 'centre on the hour' mark, a barbershop quartet style produced the words, 'Who's that running over the hill? It's Ricky Foster. It's Ricky Foster!' This really connected with what I felt, even though I'd never heard this chant before. For those of you that don't know, The Automatic's massive hit 'Monster' had inspired the rabble. Running over the hill in the song was a Monster – not a certain Mr Foster!

Dean Holden waltzed through our rearguard to reduce the deficit five minutes later, and how we held on in the final twenty, I'll never know. I'd watched the boys loads of times – one hundred and fourteen, to be precise – and in the past, I'd seen many a shocking display result in a thrashing. However, it was nice to play badly and see them win for a change. It was a match where a couple of seasons earlier we'd have lost quite comfortably through a lack of mental toughness. I could see that manager Jimmy Calderwood had begun to assemble a squad we could be proud of again.

The rival fans weren't bad, either. A couple of lads helped me to see a short cut to the station through a retail park. An old couple at Linlithgow were almost left with no option but to sprint to the capital for a show at the Usher Hall had the guard not caught the door as it closed on them. To calm their nerves, they interrogated me about what I'd been doing that afternoon.

On the penultimate leg home, I desperately wanted to assist a lovely lady with her luggage down the stairs and onto the train, but I was beaten to the punch by a besotted pensioner whose attempts beggared belief. I prayed that there were no breakables in her suitcase, because she might have sued otherwise! Former Aberdeen coach Ian Porterfield's son-in-law, draped in all the Celtic gear, surprised me getting off at Dunbar with his toddler, on the way to Sunderland. I guessed that it would take another two hours before, with the youngster tucked up in bed, he could put his feet up and reflect on the 2-1 win claimed at Parkhead over relegation-threatened Dunfermline. Whether he was, or whether he wasn't, part of the Porterfield clan, there was no point in distrusting him.

After being on the go for nearly ten hours, a Mr Chappell in his taxi made sure that I arrived safely at the Horn Inn around the back of eight, for the price of a crisp twenty-pound note.

Once hitting the sack, I felt chuffed with my attitude, knowing that I'd had the get-up-and-go to make life a little more exciting and enjoyable than it normally was, even if just for one day. Nobody would have been bothered if I had skipped a game which three years previously I wouldn't have gone to on my own, and would certainly not have enquired about the possibility of my going anyway. Back then I would have found some excuse not to go. My favourite justification? Having a slight disability made me feel vulnerable – exposing myself to all that prospective violence from antagonist aficionados, particularly considering our casuals' history. I wasn't proposing or initiating any anarchy, but nonetheless, with a cargo of booze devoured, who knows how a number of those psychotic hooligans might react to me.

The second act on this flight of rediscovery came a week and a half later – on a Tuesday night at Fir Park, Lanarkshire. It was a rearranged fixture against Motherwell in the league. After passing up an earlier, longer, coastal-route tour of the Borders, I hopped on the school bus at five to four. It bewildered me to think about how far scores of the brood on board travelled for an education. A large percentage of the pupils spent approximately ninety minutes a day being picked up and dropped off. It probably didn't inconvenience a lot of the rascals – many of whom seemed to have their own coping mechanisms for the boredom. Some things just never change, I thought, when a familiar face got on at Chirnside. She'd definitely lost a lot of weight since the last time I'd seen her. It was hard to accept that we were going to be perpetually at different ends of the social spectrum, no matter how much water had passed under the bridge following our High School exodus. Dismounting your high horse and leaving the ego behind means that maturity sets in quicker, but there are those who won't ever grow up. What's wrong with being polite and showing an interest in a fellow peer's progress after adolescence? I quite like hearing every single one of the invigorating incidents ex-classmates tell on reuniting. Insufficient endeavour made by this girl to break down the barricades was her loss, not mine.

Two rituals are carried out on matchdays. Spending a few quid predicting the correct scoreline and first goalscorer (no more than a modest pound on each), and then wasting twenty pence to use the station loo even if I don't need a pee! I find the scheme of paying a small sum for the privilege of emptying one's bladder through habit, and not inclination, to be absolutely comical. The Human Rights Commission in Strasbourg must take a look in and overrule such a daft duty!

How lucky have I been with my bets? Let's not be shy about this. Over the course of seven matches from the season just finished, I've pulled off a tidy profit margin by securing odds of 6/1 and 8/1 for away wins at Hearts and Kilmarnock respectively. This even stopped me looking at how far in you are during a particular game, as whatever will be, will be. Nothing I do or say off my own bat will transform the result. Vocal support from fans can have a major effect on their team's performance, although the men wearing the jerseys need to boast a pride in professionalism for themselves first and foremost, before those they entertain. Possessing aptitude to deliver the goods comes next. Why, then, have I never collected on a goalscorer? It's because our strikers are too inconsistent! At the end of the day it's only a bit of fun, so I don't really care who grabs the goals – as long as we win!

Once again, I met some weird and wonderful people along the way. An American tycoon on business lasting three days, accompanied by his London counterpart, was a dazzling diversion to block out my pessimistic philosophy of where we were going to blow the chance to bolster our hold on third place. As they gathered their belongings to get off at Edinburgh Waverley my fellow Englishman put Bon Jovi in mind with a defiant: 'Have a bit of faith, son!'

I feel quite blessed that this kind of encounter occurs with such frequency. I usually find something to take from the phantoms that I briefly acquaint. Seeing an Asian female and Afro-Caribbean woman sitting together at a table across the aisle heightened my approval of the mixed-race country that we live in. They were like chalk and cheese – the hippie, Mrs Bob Marley, ready to cause a stir and break all the rules, and her partner in crime, the oppressed refugee guinea pig, selected to be one half of a convenient arranged marriage that very few escape. Two sassy Scotch stunners sat adjacent to me till every one of us had to evacuate to the flanking suburbs. Well, I'm saying stunners, but one was old enough to be my granny, and she actually gave me meticulous guidelines to Glasgow Queen Street from Glasgow Central for on the way home. I certainly needed not to get lost in the wee small hours, in a place of which I had no prior knowledge, and her tips reassured me that everything was going to be okay. Whether it was just the circumstances I found myself in, or whether something was subconsciously tapping into my deepest darkest fantasies, I'm not quite sure, but the attraction I felt towards the other lady bamboozled me somewhat. I never normally went for her kind. I couldn't take my eyes off the hair – her captivating auburn collage (whatever the proper name for this charismatic style is) drawing me in.

A tickly throat in full swing struck me from nowhere, and if not for the bottle of Oasis Fruit Juices bought at the newsagents, a special episode of Beauty And The Geek would have been commissioned on my behalf. Almost choking to death every two or three minutes made me come across as a bit of a fool. Gazing out of the window at the countryside to disguise the uneasiness only made things worse, as built-up water, streaming down my cheeks, ultimately gave the game away.

Mind you, I may plot to kill the next driver that goes through the Carstairs stop so slowly! It's freaky to think that somewhere close lies a facility where all the criminally insane who, for their own good and society's safety, are locked away.

It saddened me, walking up the steps where a Red Rooster Taxi should have been waiting at the front entrance to whisk me to the stadium, and knowing that I'd probably never see that smartly-dressed woman again. I'd booked the taxi by phone earlier that day, so there were no excuses for it not being there! I wondered about whether they really thought that this was the way to run a business. Your reputation in any trade speaks volumes. Yes? If you are lagging behind fellow competitors because of ineptitude, you only have yourself to blame. Standards must be maintained. As a bald-headed shabby-looking middle-aged bloke – holdall over one shoulder, guitar case in the opposite hand – lurked purposefully, I wished my taxi would burn rubber a little quicker and drop me at the notorious 'peeing' phone box. In fact, the man was quite compassionate – supporting my suspicions about entering 'the lion's den'. By that, I mean it wasn't just football thugs who petrified me, but those on the street who looked like an 'average Joe', too. There are several districts in Motherwell where you just don't go after a certain time of day. I can't believe that these places still exist.

There's no need for life to be that sinister.

I'm not saying that every female who attends a match on the road is a born-and-bred Aberdonian. However, the North-East man has pretty good taste in the fairer sex. Some of the beauties I've seen at grounds are absolute crackers. To grasp why they've come to the football at all is beyond me. Surely a trip round the High Street stores is more appealing? It's got to be that they come to see these perfect physiques that are preserved by hours spent at the gym between training. I think that 'Ladette' is the wrong word to use. They are especially noticeable when players get cautioned for audaciously ripping off their shirts to celebrate a goal – revealing a little more than they should. There has certainly been an increase in the number of women attending games in the last few years.

It's a pity I've not identified a possible target to be my new partner. I read an article in the paper once, which said that the sexiest men came from Manchester and the dullest from Cardiff. I've often dreamed of seeing a sexy girl wake up 'the morning after the night before' with nothing on but that distinctive red shirt belonging to me, as she jumps on my sofa and asks for coffee and a slice of toast, anticipating an early bath. (Didn't feel the X-Factor to impress the damsel in distress on the train. So, she's another that slipped through the net.) I'd be keen to charm a future girlfriend in the amazing ambience that's inserted fear into many a team across Europe on more than one occasion.

That evening, the setting had an extremely moving edge to it. Singing 'One Man Went To Mow, Went To Mow A Mea-dow' is like performing a version of the 'Haka'. This intense tribal war dance has been given legendary status because of those fellas they call the All Blacks – who can bring panic to countless opponents throughout the planet who are thrown in at the deep end with a side that can make the sport of Rugby look so effortless. But the players don't have the weight of a whole country on their shoulders and we don't give a toss (dry wit I'm told) about whether we win or not, as we're there for a laugh, and winning's an additional benefit.

Discouragingly, nobody I knew was able to appreciate my contentment on returning. My resurrection had finally come – fresh buoyancy, shifting me closer to enlightenment. I paid only nine pounds to take a seat of my choice in the middle of the radical rebels. I had shown my disability travel concessionary card to the man behind the turnstile, who mistook it for a student pass. Lightning struck twice when I was told to advance to the club shop to get change for a programme – just like at Falkirk. The cost of the twenty-four fifty train ticket straight to my destination had been money well spent.

A fortunate 2-0 victory set us up nicely for our Govan arch-rivals at Pittodrie three days later – in one of the biggest affairs to be staged at headquarters for several years. Rookie Andrew Considine's optimistic punt upfield, resulting in Marc Fitzpatrick's 34th minute O.G., broke the deadlock, and Lee Miller's agile far-post knock-back was perfect cannon-fodder for Ricky Foster to settle proceedings. This versatile midfielder's 22-yard second-half injury time screamer instigated a booming 'Bring on the Rangers!' that raised the roof, as we emptied the park, happy as Larry.

Owing to my recent feelings of bliss, I knew that life was improving, in more ways than one. I needed things to look forward to in order for the Nile smile to remain. Yet again, my taxi returning me to the station caused a lot of confusion with the driver – who was supposed to be picking up someone with a different surname from the one I gave! There must only be a certain number of phone cubicles outside a sporting arena within spitting distance of a car showroom, particularly in Motherwell! On the other hand, forking out under a fiver, or four pounds ten to be precise, is a paltry amount, to ensure my personal protection – no matter how long, or by what means, it takes to get to the institution.

Popping into the loos before unavoidable uncharted territory, I came across three lads who backed up the artistic instructions of Thomas the Tank Engine, Clarence and Annabelle in the shed, written down by my surrogate grandmother on a page taken from the Daily Record's PM edition. I convinced myself that I'd met Gordon in a past life – his accent reminded me of somebody I knew from Inverness. Stewart looked like a carbon copy of somebody that had been sent to help, with my line of attack being a fugitive attempting to flee the scene of the crime in one piece. He had left a small village near Selkirk, called Midlem, to enrol at Glasgow University, so maybe I've seen him out of the corner of my eye whilst watching my brother play football for Duns Juniors! Iain was the first to introduce himself, and he called his flatmate, Katy, to see if she wanted to celebrate the triumph with a few drinks at the union they often frequented. It appeared from Gordon's reaction to Katy's declining Iain's spontaneous suggestion that the man didn't have a great deal of success with women. I couldn't see why, though – he wasn't exactly ugly. I found that smelling an assortment of continental dishes, and alluding to the striking structural design along enclosed lanes, took my mind off possible dangers that lingered in the shadows.

There were two buses – scattered inside with the odd person here and there. A randy couple's demonstration at the foot of a tower block (controlled by an intercom) was clearly oblivious of anything or anybody, and provoked the same kind of feeling as you can get when you walk in on your parents going at it hammer and tongs. Not a happy sight!

Pieces written by journalists that claim to be 'everything you need to know for a fulfilling sex life' have me in hysterics. Avant-garde single women must find it so confusing, and yet so absorbing, to learn the tricks of the trade from those who've supposedly seen a thing or two. But it's those who are joined at the hip and reaching their Golden Jubilee who are the best trendsetters. You will have seen the spreads stating 'never to go to bed on an argument' or 'keeping alive the fun beneath the sheets the older you get' is key to making a relationship work.

I was quite surprised by how, at eleven o'clock on a weekday night, there were so many travellers using the Glasgow to Edinburgh line. In fact, a six- or seven-year-old delectable fair-haired girl, who was full of vigour and curiosity, obliterated my feelings of restlessness. My brother and I were never allowed to stay up that late on a school night, you know! Just hearing her talking made me feel tired. Two gentlemen who were sitting at the same table as I was, offered little in the way of conversation, which is why I tried to look as if I was amusing myself by flicking through the match programme, pretending to fill my brain with interesting data. I'm sure the one who was slumped in his seat slipped in and out of consciousness, while the other was immersed in a paper. I made it my responsibility not to kick Sleeping Beauty's feet or rustle Max Clifford's preferred reading material. I did manage to have a blether with someone who seemed to be everybody's exquisite PR guru, and gave a hush-hush exclusive on the man sitting right beside him.

It's no wonder that the general public has such a strained liaison with the boys in blue, when continuously met with complete and utter contempt – like I was at Waverley by two bobbies, just because I couldn't find the lift to my humble abode in 'buzzer round' mode. It had just touched midnight, so I wasn't really in the mood to take any of their rubbish. Would a cooling-down period in the cells for a bit of petulance have been the funniest moment of my life? Instead of kipping at my brother Paul's flat and catching a bus the following morning, I'd arranged for a couple of lads to collect me outside the station – only having to pay twenty pounds in petrol money for their services.

Basking in the glory of seeing my team win yet another game was okay, yet all I really wanted to do was fall into bed in front of the telly before catching some shut-eye. Flames from the gas fire provided not just heat but the idyllic source of light that I worshipped. It brought a certain relaxing atmosphere – which, if there was nothing decent on the box, added to the mood for me, and I could doze off to songs selected randomly by the five-disc CD player, almost as soon as my head hit the pillow.

The drivers – Durham (real name Paul) and Suttle (Scott) – were folk I knew from Duns, who relished the change of scene on offer. Being a lot older means I'm not exactly a mate, but just someone who seems to have a grand affinity with a section of the town's youth. I hunted for a fish supper. I was so hungry. But even at half past twelve in the urban underground, every takeaway we passed was closed. We lost our senses in Dalkeith and settled for some Original Doritos chips, a bag of Minstrels and bottle of Blackcurrant Oasis at Fordel's 24HR garage. I even got my chauffeur and his aide packets of Salt and Vinegar and Cheese and Onion crisps as a tiny thank-you – though not the pint of lager, as they were driving, remember! We stopped for a break, halfway up Soutra Hill, and the Aussie soap, 'Neighbours', entered my head as for a moment I struggled to believe there were associates about who would do such a favour for me at an unsociable hour.

Back home, I jumped under the covers with seconds to spare clutching a large bar of Dairy Milk Chocolate. It was just after one in the morning, and I watched 'The War at Home' – an American comedy about the struggles of bringing up three teenage kids. 'You've done it once, you can do it a million times now' is how it goes... No? Well, this is what I thought.

It had depended entirely on travel arrangements, but if truth were told, I had illustrated desire for the Motherwell game in a way that I've rarely ignited in the past.

In January of the same year, I planned to attend two matches within forty-eight hours – a televised Scottish Cup Third Round Replay on the Thursday at Easter Road against Hibernian, and then a league meeting at Fir Park with Motherwell on the Saturday. Sadly, the latter was postponed, due to a waterlogged pitch. Having been a goal in front and then spanked 4-1, I saw the Motherwell clash (screened by Setanta as opposed to Sky Sports) as the perfect tonic.

The club themselves were raging at all concerned for failing to show the common sense to put back the fixture till the Sunday. I wouldn't have minded stretching my mini-tour with Aberdeen another day longer – even though I was choked with the cold.

The third and final phase of this tale unfolded at Rugby Park, Kilmarnock – on the last day in March. It followed a heavy defeat to Rangers in the brawl at Ibrox, and then a narrow victory over the nearest challengers, Hearts, a week later.

I made my familiar preparations, and this time, instead of dropping me off at the station, Mum left me at Chisholm's, so that I could first place a wager on the game. I was feeling extremely woozy due to a lack of sleep coupled with an upset stomach. My mate, Joseph, couldn't understand why I'd chosen the hard labour of a double shift surveying a bunch of fleecing scoundrels on sickening salaries, who for their livelihoods ran round a field kicking a bit of leather. He diagnosed insanity. Maybe he would have seen where I was coming from had it been a woman I was going to all this trouble for… But yes, I'd planned to cruise the Ayrshire plains and Border countryside nigh on twelve hours just to see how our Euro credentials were holding up.

As I bought my travel ticket, I learned that my train was nine minutes behind schedule because of a technical fault. This seemed okay, as now I would have less time to wait at Glasgow Central. But later, a voice coming through the speakers informed me that the delay would be forty-five minutes, and I knew that I would miss my connection to Kilmarnock. Mum had given me thirty-seven pounds and ninety pence as an early birthday present so that I could afford this journey, and I approached the Fat Controller for a solution to the problem. Fortunately there was an alternative, and I got to the game just in time.

Noisy, inebriated supporters and the inevitable police reaction threatened to wreak havoc. It was deafening, but I didn't want them to be apprehended on arriving at the ground, and was on the edge of my seat, inwardly begging the law to employ a little discretion, as they were causing nobody any harm.

This game was to be my maiden win at the venue. It was only my second visit here. Faded memories of a 3-1 drubbing from the mid-nineties flooded back as I frantically strived to establish residency on the virtually-full Red Dwarf glider. The strangest difference I noticed was how much closer the troops seemed on the field compared with what I recalled of this as a child. I was no nearer or further away on this occasion – so maybe the stand had shrunk… I don't know!

Pressed against the ropes and gasping for air, Don King's bland bout exploded out of nowhere in fifty-nine minutes – two uppercuts rocking the challengers' confidence at a pivotal point in the match. James Fowler and keeper Graeme Smith got their wires crossed trying to clear veteran Craig Brewster's jab towards goal. Gary Dempsey, the intended target, watched in delight when Smith attempting to punch was made to look a fool. Fowler then looped a header up and over Killie's last line of resistance into the unguarded net. This score of 1-0 subsequently became 2-0 – Scott Severin doing the damage, as Darren Mackie took his well-measured free kick on the chest with aplomb. Captain Marvel Russell Anderson prodded in the assailant's layoff from close range, and this silenced the critics who had reckoned that we lacked the kind of steely sector in our strategy that was required to challenge the Old Firm's impressive trophy-haul dominating the domestic scene since the late '80s and early '90s, and beyond. Zander Diamond's handball howler after eighty-six minutes presented Steven Naismith and Killie with a way back into the game from the penalty spot – which Scotland's newest recruit dispatched cool as a cucumber. Finally, the referee blew the whistle, and the game was finished.

The journey to Glasgow Central had me quaking in my boots. Rowdy revellers and some Russian factory workers – who were joyous at Aberdeen winning the adulation of more neutrals – were being watched by the local constabulary. The latter group weren't taking any chances either way. Even if the odds were stacked against us we'd have given our 'foreign' friends a run for their money had events escalated! I'd have been the sneaky 'spectator' – tripping people up as they went for somebody else! I may not have brute force, but there's something between my ears if folk should care to take a look once in a while.

I made getting to Glasgow Queen Street a mountain out of a molehill – confusing the trail put together by a Glasgow Central officer patrolling entry onto the premises! Then everyone piled on the train – like animals were marching aboard the Ark, two by two. Will and Sean were no different. They were too dapper and well-spoken to be Blue Noses. Will tickled my taste buds when leaving some of his Chicken Pakora in its wrapper. The aroma sucked me in, and instead of the usual King Rib Supper, I opted to order some for myself at Crolla's Fish and Chicken Bar near Galashiels Bus Station.

I had caught the X95 in Edinburgh's depot where I could make it home earlier free of charge by using that badge again. But I became very agitated – biting my lip in the company of a really stuck-up female who got on. Never before had I wanted two Teddy Bears in the form of Will and Sean to keep me occupied than when confronted with this sorry excuse for a woman – a Posh Spice wannabe. It was a shame really – considering that I'd have much preferred talking to her pal, who was the spitting image of Nadine Coyle of Girls Aloud fame, and seemed a lot more grounded than Madame herself. I couldn't get a word in edgeways, since she was so self-absorbed in her own illusion of what the boyfriend's role should be when it came to organising their wedding. I guessed that his side of the family would probably cough up in terms of the big day expenses. They do say love's blind, eh? Please join me in wishing luck to this bloke – whoever he is – because by the time the gold digger's finished with him, he's going to need a good lawyer!

This was bad enough, but then I saw that a prat who had boarded at the same stop seemed to be showing off his physique. Some people are just too hung up on physical perfection. I accept there are those who want to look after themselves, but it doesn't mean that everyone has to look like this, and surely what's inside counts for something? Unfortunately the way mankind is, and the way mankind should be, are two totally different entities.

Going to these three matches and forgetting about my hemiplegia and the two centimetres of brain damage that comes with it, and also the epilepsy and its pitfalls, was a blessing in disguise. Now and then, I just don't want to deal with my out-of-control wavy strands of hair, mismatched teeth, lack of style in dressing to impress or the subject of money for that matter. Actually, I'm worth much more than that. Shall I let you into a little secret? I wore trainers throughout this football feast that were too small for me and had holes in them. What a tramp I am! Wonder if anybody noticed? Leaky sneakers, but I've made giant strides for the better during the month of March. Can one treasure oneself on the inside, and at the same time feel like a freak of nature on the outside? I do, but I'll let you decide.

Susan (who's actually my step-auntie but prefers me not to use that word in front of others) picked me up off the submarine machine (First's single-decker) at Gala. Her brother, Gordon, is mum's husband. As gratitude for getting me out of a sticky situation, I paid for a couple of pints to be left behind the stable at the Horn Inn when Susan next went in. See, I do know the way to a woman's heart! But something's just come back to me... Susan gave me money to buy her a smoked sausage at Crolla's.

I hope that all my observations from beginning to end have rung a bell, as my intentions when I gave this particular account a title were to show that I can write about my favourite temptation and give myself a more defining meaning within it.

I want to add that eight days after the Kilmarnock game, an acquaintance of mine in Duns killed himself on Easter Sunday. The tragedy left me utterly devastated, and I don't think I'll ever comprehend what happened. He had sworn to me two days before the catastrophe that he wasn't going to let the hit parade win anymore. Since I'd just proved to everybody that I'm not a loose cannon – so that anything's possible – I was very sad that this person hadn't made it. This is why I want to dedicate this piece of writing to all those who made this win happen and to the only man other than my Granddad to ever call me 'Cocker'. Wherever you are now, buddy, I hope you're happy.

Another thing I wanted to do was to mention what I'd learnt about myself from the whole fling. I had the idea of tying the reality of three victories in three weeks, with me scoring a hat-trick every striker dreams of – a goal with his right foot, one with his left foot and then one with the head.

Being comfortable in my own company is a primary consideration. There'll always be times when nobody's around and individual happiness is down to me and me alone. I would have loved to share my hat-trick experience with somebody I know well. My brother Paul or comrade Dave would have been fine. More people ought to want the pleasure of my alliance because I'm good to be around, and have lots to offer. However, if I had gone to just one of these matches with a bodyguard there'd have been no scope to write this saga, as I would have been less taken up with my observations of people while I was out and about.

People may question my validity in the football fan bracket, but it's had a major part to play in my life, and always will. It's the only consistent thing I've had of my own throughout the heartache of the last nineteen years, and that's got to be worth celebrating.

Do I want to pass the lance down to a next of kin? Funny you should ask me that. Every time someone's mentioned the subject, I've insisted that fatherhood is not for me.

'Hat-Trick' has taken me several months to compile. It was important to me to give it time to emerge spontaneously, and variety of vocabulary is an absolute necessity. Sometimes I found myself writing at five and six in the morning, when nothing can disturb me.

Then I had a dream about becoming a dad, and it freaked me out. The identity of the mother was unclear, but I know that the child was a boy because I kept repeating his name – Rory Seymour – in my head, to make it feel real. I pined for a daughter called Renee before waking – which was rather baffling. I freshened up in the bathroom wondering what the heck it meant, and then set a deadline to finish this story by the time of my fairly imminent dentist appointment.

I want to thank my doctor, Gordon Sim, for prescribing me the verve to complete this final furlong of my book, and for his continued support. I sometime think that I must have driven him to the brink of retirement with my ranting on awkward topics such as whether the increasing size of a mole on my back meant I had skin cancer, or the inability to get it up for a spot of hanky panky made me feel inadequate as a man. There had been a few snide comments around here about how I hadn't shaved or groomed (as I struggled to write this final piece) and so I felt it necessary to see my GP twice in the space of four days to talk things through. I told him how I was very stressed at people having no faith in me. He told me to have some self-belief and that he'd be first in the queue to get a signed copy of my book once it was published!

I do remember how in 'Mind Games' I promised not to mention Aberdeen Football Club again. However, I felt compelled to write about my hat-trick voyage soon after our robbery at Kilmarnock, and more so following my chum's death.

By getting my name out there, I am determined to prove that those who doubt me are wrong. God loves a trier, and trying is something that people can't take away from me. I fight to keep my right to live life the way I see fit. This might not be the 'correct' way, but it is my own way. There should be no need to feel inferior to people ever again. SeaBass has finally KICKED ASS! Not before time, too.

I hope that you've enjoyed this journal. Everyone's something special. I'm somebody special, because I'm letting people know of my feeling that I'm a genius – no? We'll be here till the next lunar eclipse if I explain why, so I'm not going to. Done enough of that in the past and it's got me nowhere. If others disagree, then they're the ones who'll ultimately miss out. Accept what I say as the truth, and we can move on to bigger and better things.

Also available from Augur Press

Beyond the Veil by Mirabelle Maslin	£8.99	0-9549551-4-5
Fay by Mirabelle Maslin	£8.99	0-9549551-3-7
Carl and other writings by Mirabelle Maslin	£5.99	0-9549551-2-9
Letters to my Paper Lover by Fleur Soignon	£7.99	0-9549551-1-0
On a Dog Lead by Mirabelle Maslin	£6.99	978-0-9549551-5-1
Poems of Wartime Years by W N Taylor	£4.99	978-0-9549551-6-8
For ages 8-14 years (and adult readers too): Tracy by Mirabelle Maslin	£6.95	0-9549551-0-2

Postage and packing – £1.00 per title

Ordering:
By phone   +44 (0) 131 440 1690
By post   Delf House, 52, Penicuik Road, Roslin, Midlothian
             EH25 9LH   UK
By fax   +44 (0) 131 448 0990
By e-mail   info@augurpress.com
Online   www.augurpress.com   (credit cards accepted)

Cheques payable to Augur Press

Prices and availability subject to change without notice

When placing your order, please mention if you do not wish to receive any additional information

www.augurpress.com

Mirabelle Maslin
ON A DOG LEAD

Mirabelle Maslin
CARL AND OTHER WRITINGS

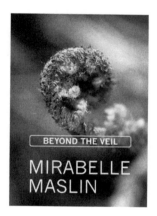

BEYOND THE VEIL

MIRABELLE
MASLIN

Letters to my Paper Lover
FLEUR SOIGNON

Poems of Wartime Years
W N Taylor

Mirabelle
Maslin

tracy

from the author of Beyond the Veil